Freddy's Book

Freddy's Book

by John Neufeld

AN AVON  CAMELOT BOOK

AVON BOOKS
A division of
The Hearst Corporation
959 Eighth Avenue
New York, New York 10019

First Camelot Printing, March, 1975.
Third Printing

Freddy's Book

1

Freddy wasn't stupid. His mother reminded him often, and strongly, that he wasn't. From time to time his father, too, admitted that Freddy had a "good head."

But standing where he stood and seeing what he saw, Freddy Alexander definitely felt that way. Dumb, silly, stupid. Curious.

And a little angry at himself, too.

The word stared back down at Freddy from the whitewashed wall. It wasn't a new word. Freddy remembered seeing it scrawled on a brick wall and once soaped on the window of a subway car in Toronto. He had even heard boys in his own class use it, laughingly. He had ignored it. If anyone had asked him if he knew what the word meant, he would have said "Sure" and hoped that he wasn't blushing.

And today, here it was again, scraped into the

paint in his new school.

Freddy zipped up his trousers and pushed the lever down hard. Then he went to a sink.

There he decided. Clearly, the only thing for it was to understand what the word meant. Once. For all. If it were going to appear in strange places, if it were going to be heard from boys his own age, he would simply have to know exactly what it meant.

He decided that whatever its meaning, the word couldn't be difficult to understand. There were only four letters in it.

Drying his hands, Freddy let the word sound through his mind. Then, very quietly, he tried it aloud. "Fuck," he whispered, feeling oddly nervous. "Fuck, fuck, fuck."

He threw the paper towel into a tall receptacle, seeing his own pink face in the mirrors over the sinks. He turned around.

The door of the boys' washroom opened. Without looking up to see who was coming towards him, Freddy began to move, fast.

He noticed as he passed that the person was much taller than he, a teacher, wearing a plaid sports jacket and gray trousers.

Freddy ran down the hall to rejoin his class.

2

Freddy didn't go home right after school. Though the temperature was below freezing, he spent some time hanging around the playground, dangling up-side down from iron bars and pushing the merry-go-round (which he had to himself) as fast as it would go before leaping aboard. There was a swift, cool wind that came up at him from the football field below. Early winter darkness followed not long after.

Finally chilled and a bit hungry, Freddy started for home. He walked with his hands deep in his parka pockets, his shoulders hunched against the weather, and a frown on his forehead. He was think-ing of his sister.

Secretly he liked Pru—even if, as today, she pretended after school not to know him and went off with a group of her giggling friends. Still, he did like her, though boys weren't supposed to get along with their sisters.

Pru was five years older than Freddy. Worse than this, she was taller.

Pru was pretty. She laughed a lot. She was always doing things that Freddy thought were exciting, although she never invited him to join in. Pru seemed to think that she and Freddy were members of two separate families; that because she was almost grown up she had to forget about her own family and spend every moment with her friends, or alone, doing "things."

Freddy wondered if, secretly, Pru liked him, too. He thought perhaps she did. For sometimes, with no real reason, Pru would look at him and smile a special smile. It was a smile that seemed to say to Freddy, "We know, don't we?" It was a smile that Freddy couldn't help returning.

Most of the time, though, Freddy wasn't sophisticated enough for Pru. "Smart" was the word she used, making it sound as though that meant the total opposite of everything she thought Freddy might be, now or ever. But Freddy forgave Pru her airs. When Pru smiled that special smile at him, he forgave everything.

Almost. There was one thing Freddy couldn't

forgive: Pru's teasing. What made Freddy angriest was that Pru laughed most at the one thing over which he had no control.

He tried. He certainly tried. Every morning, for five whole minutes, he hung from a chinning bar that extended above his head in the doorway to his room. (His mother had asked if the bar couldn't be put in his closet instead, since she and Nelly, the maid, always forgot to duck when they went into Freddy's room to clean. Freddy felt he needed the space on both sides of the bedroom door to swing.)

Still in pajamas, Freddy would climb onto a small footstool and jump up to grasp the bar with both hands. Latched onto it, he stayed there—eyes closed, breath held in, teeth clenched. Hanging there he waited, wanting to feel his backbone stretching, his legs growing, his arms lengthening. (He sometimes wondered if this was really the very best thing to do. Suppose his arms grew and nothing else did?)

Every few seconds, he would open his eyes to look at his bedside clock. When it was time, he simply let go the bar and dropped to the floor. Every morning he felt taller. The next morning, he would know he wasn't. Reaching the bar was just as difficult as it had been the day before.

Hanging wasn't all Freddy did. He ate liver. He even liked it a little.

And, often as he remembered, Freddy walked through doorways reaching up. His father had told him that this, too, might help. You walked through the doorway, stopped, and reached up as far as you could with one hand. Not on tiptoes, but flatfooted. Then, as you went through another doorway, you did the same, only with the other hand measuring the frame.

"Tweenie" was what Pru called her brother. "Tweenie" Alexander. The name made Freddy boil. Sometimes he pointed out that Pru herself wasn't any giant. But Pru had an answer for that. Girls, she said, were supposed to be small. "Petite," she had told him. Freddy hated that word, too.

Being around Pru sometimes made Freddy envy Johnny Norman. Johnny's family always seemed to be doing things together and, even better, seemed to be having fun doing them. Not that Freddy was ashamed of his own family. He just wished it were more like the families he read about. The Normans, for example, had cookouts. They had spelling bees when it rained. They went fishing together on Saturday mornings, early. This year, Johnny had told him, he was going to be let out of school for two whole weeks so that he could go with his family to Florida.

But Pru stood apart from activities like these. Rarely would she do what someone else suggested. She always had her reasons. There were special things she just had to do instead.

But it wasn't only Pru who kept the Alexanders from being the family of Freddy's dreams. Freddy's father was too often away on business. It seemed to Freddy that when someone had a wonderful idea for an outing, either Pru said no or their father was in Detroit or Chicago. Mr. Alexander talked about taking a month off some summer so the family could take a motor tour—across Canada when they had lived there; now across the United States—but he never did. Business was always just too heavy.

When he *was* home, Freddy's father had so much catching up to do with Pru and Freddy and their mother that when at last he did know all the news, it was time for him to leave again for Minneapolis or Kansas City.

Although the time he and his father spent together made Freddy happy, he felt more and more pushed, as though he had to find ways to please his father quickly, to show him affection before another trip took him away. He wanted his father to know that he, Freddy, was exactly what his father thought he was, what he wanted him to be. Although, from time to time, Freddy wondered whether he was, in fact, exactly what his father wanted him to be.

3

"Hey, Moose!"

"Freddy!"

Both calls mixed in Freddy's ears. He turned and saw, at curbside, David Trafton's car.

David leaned across his girlfriend, Tina, and waved at Freddy through the window. Freddy smiled and waved back and walked to the car.

"How's the trickiest defensive back in town?" David asked, reaching out to tousle Freddy's brown hair. "All set for the big one?"

Freddy nodded and grinned.

"Get a good night's rest," Tina said, smiling down at Freddy. "Not too much late television."

"I'm not allowed up past nine," said Freddy seriously.

David sat up again and revved his motor. "Moose," he shouted over the roar of his engine, "tomorrow everyone plays!"

Tina turned and looked adoringly at David, and then turned back to Freddy to wave good-by. David's car slid away from the curb, sounding like one of the motorboats Freddy remembered hearing on summer mornings at Murray Bay. Freddy watched the car, trying to remember—since his friends thought it important—what kind of car, exactly, David Trafton was driving. What kind of car, in fact, anyone drove. But he couldn't. All he could see in the darkness was the blue-and-white DRAKE U. on the back window of the car, before it rounded a corner. Freddy turned back towards the sidewalk, thinking about what David had said.

"Tomorrow everyone plays," David had announced. All season Freddy had been sitting on the bench. Small and fast, but ready, he had never been signaled into a game.

After a while, Freddy had even forgotten most of the plays he had memorized during practice. He had written them down, diagraming his own moves and positions. But as the season progressed, Freddy's interest had waned. It seemed to him he didn't have much to do anyway, except stay out of the way. That was probably what David had had in mind when he assigned Freddy to his position.

Freddy had not played football in Canada. Playing it now, in Iowa, was his father's idea. It was American, it was fun, it was a way of making friends fast. It was good exercise, it would teach sportsmanship, and—besides—Americans just didn't play soccer. (Freddy knew this was true. He had not yet seen boys his own age even kicking a soccer ball around just for fun.)

Busy pushing his breath out in front of him, then watching it rise and disappear above his head, Freddy almost walked past his own driveway. He turned off the sidewalk and moved up the cement that ran alongside the cream-yellow frame house. Darkness was almost complete but for streetlamps and a few early stars. The wind had risen and the temperature had dropped.

"Well," Nelly said as she saw him stamping his feet on the mat inside the kitchen door. "You certainly took your time getting home."

Freddy hugged himself for warmth and then threw his coat and gloves and scarf on a chair. "Where's Mom?" he asked.

"Out socializing," said Nelly abruptly, turning her back to Freddy to go back to her work.

Freddy watched her as she stood at the sink

cleaning vegetables. Nelly always made him feel as though he had forgotten to do something she had asked him to do. Maybe she just didn't like him. He wondered why.

"That sister of yours called, too," Nelly said, scraping carrots rhythmically. "I'm laying out dinner just the same. If it's cold when everyone gets here, that's just tough luck. Friday never comes soon enough for me."

Freddy walked to Nelly's side. "How come you're unhappy?" he asked.

Nelly spun away from the sink, the scraper still in her hand. "Now, just listen here," she said. Then she seemed to change her mind about what she had begun to say. She forced her face into a smile. "That's just the way I talk, boy," she said. "Don't pay attention to the *way* I say things. Only to *what* I say."

Freddy thought that if he smiled back at her, perhaps Nelly would realize that *he* didn't dislike *her*. "Our teacher says that when you listen, you can sometimes hear more than just words."

Nelly stood without moving. Then she nodded, more to herself than to Freddy. "She's right," she said, "and you, you're just too smart for your own good." Her smile broadened and seemed more real. Freddy was pleased.

But having mentioned a teacher, and thinking then of school, Freddy remembered suddenly he had some research to do.

"Where you off to now?" Nelly asked as Freddy turned away from her and walked out of the room.

"I have to go take a fuck," he replied in as deep a voice as he could produce. He disappeared around the door into the dining room.

Nelly stood stock-still. Her mouth opened. She started to speak but couldn't. Instead, she began to laugh.

Freddy peered out from around the door, feeling somehow disappointed. He didn't know what he had expected, but he certainly hadn't expected Nelly to laugh.

4

Freddy looked around his room. He didn't feel like doing anything special. There wasn't time, really, to begin anything before dinner.

He walked farther into the room and lay down on his bed, looking at the posters along the wall above his head. They were from the fair he had been taken to when he was little more than a baby. His family had driven from Toronto to Montreal to stay with an aunt. They had spent an entire week roaming the clean, bright streets of the islands where the fair had been.

What Freddy could remember of that time were only odd things. The funny-looking houses of foreign countries like Ethiopia and Japan. The sensation of standing atop the Canadian Pavilion, leaning against its glass walls and looking down into the fairgrounds, feeling the whole building being shaken by strong, gusty hot winds that swept up from the river, seemingly directed at him alone.

And with this, he remembered being perched atop his father's shoulders, seeming taller than the rest of the world put together, hanging on to his father's ears for dear life as they threaded their way among the crowds bustling in one hundred different directions at the same time.

Idly, Freddy wondered if he would ever hold a little boy that way. Mr. Alexander was taller than six feet, and although he swore to Freddy that as a boy he had been the runt of his class, Freddy felt his father said that only to make him feel better. To keep Freddy hoping and trying.

Going to the fair had been fun, Freddy decided, lying on his back, eyes wide open and unblinking. It would be nice, he thought, if someone else at his new school had been there, too, so that together they could talk about it and match memories. Johnny Norman—even though he was supposed to go to Florida—had never been farther away from home than a place called Lake Okoboji, which didn't sound all that exciting to Freddy.

Thinking about Johnny brought a faint scowl to Freddy's face. Johnny always knew everything. Nothing surprised him. He could always have told you so if only you had asked.

Freddy stood up and went into his parents' room. He picked up the telephone and dialed Johnny's number. He waited a moment. "Hello," he said. "Is Johnny home?"

"It *is* me, dummy!" Johnny answered.

"Oh," Freddy said. "Hi."

"Hi yourself," Johnny mimicked. "What's going on?"

"Nothing much. I was just wondering . . ."

"What?"

"Well," Freddy hesitated, hating to ask because he just *knew* Johnny would have the right answer. "Do you know what 'fuck' means?"

"Sure," Johnny replied. "Everybody does."

"What?"

"Well," Johnny said, stretching the word carefully. "What it is," he said after a minute, "is bumping."

"Bumping?" Freddy was puzzled. "What do you mean?"

"I don't know," Johnny admitted, "but that's what it is. I heard some older guys at school talk about bumping someone. One of the girls in their class. Bumping the hell out of her, they said."

"That sounds dumb," Freddy said.

"You're the one who's dumb, Freddy. You're the one who didn't know."

"Are you sure?" insisted Freddy. "Just bumping into somebody?"

"Of course I'm sure," came the firm reply. "What did you think it meant?"

"I thought maybe it had something to do with going to the bathroom."

Johnny considered this a moment. "No," he said, "it's just something people write on bathroom walls."

"That's a pretty dumb thing to do," declared Freddy.

"Yeah, I guess it is. What are you doing after supper?"

Freddy knew he was not allowed to play out of doors after dark. Besides, it was too cold to want to play there, anyway. "My dad's away," he said. "I have to stay in and keep my mother company."

"Ech!" Johnny said. "I guess I'll see you tomorrow, then."

"I guess so. Bye."

"Bye," said Johnny.

Freddy put the phone down and thought a

minute. It didn't make any sense at all. Just bumping into someone couldn't be much fun. And if whatever it was wasn't fun, why would people be so interested in it? Then again, he had never tried bumping. Maybe he should, before deciding anything seriously.

He went back to his own room to get ready for dinner. Freddy wondered whether Pru had ever been bumped. Since she was always trying to be very trendy, Freddy supposed she probably had. He wondered why she hadn't ever said anything about it.

5

Freddy couldn't concentrate. Dinner had made him sleepy. He looked at the books on his desk, knowing that if he could bring himself to finish the assignments from school now he would be free the rest of the weekend.

He wished his father were home from his trip. When he was, Freddy rushed through his homework so that he and his father could go down into the basement to work on something electric with tools and wires and control panels.

Freddy's father was an electrical engineer. While what this meant had long ago been explained to Freddy, all he had retained in his mind was the word "electrical." It was a magic word. Almost everything that was fun seemed to need electricity: his trains, his model cars, the television set.

Freddy laid down his pencil and looked out the window. The lights from the kitchen were still on, shining out into the night beneath him. His mother was probably having another cup of tea as she cleaned the dishes. Nelly had long since left.

Freddy smiled a little. What a dumb thing, he thought. Bumping. Then he smiled a little more broadly.

He stood up and closed his books. Opening his own door, he stepped into the hall and walked a few steps.

Freddy didn't knock on Pru's door. Instead, he started to open it, very slowly, and then rushed it past the spot where it always squeaked and gave him away.

Pru was sitting with her back towards him, bent over her own work on her desk. All Freddy could see were her dark brown hair covering the top of her sweater and her stockinged feet crossed at the ankles beneath her chair.

He walked in, tiptoeing to her side.

"Oh!" gasped Pru, whirling around. "You scared me to death! Didn't anyone ever teach you to knock?"

"I didn't want to bother you," Freddy said.

"Then what are you doing here at all, you tweenie?"

"Don't call me that," Freddy said. "I don't call you names."

"Of course you don't," Pru announced, pushing back her chair. "You wouldn't dare. I'd wipe you out."

Freddy spread his legs a little and deepened his voice. "Big talk," he said.

"You don't think I can?" Pru asked threateningly. Slowly she stood up.

"You couldn't even catch me to do it," Freddy challenged, an even voice hiding his excitement. He backed away from her. Just a little.

Pru smiled down at her brother. "Is that why you came in here? To pick a fight?"

Freddy looked steadily back at her. "Well, no . . . and yes," he said. He took another step backward.

Pru watched him for a second. Then she lunged out after him, her arms spread wide to catch him, to pin his arms to his sides and then spank him when he was helpless.

Freddy stood his ground. In fact, he took a step towards her as she came at him.

"Got you!" Pru cried happily.

Freddy grinned up at her. "Nope," he said "I just got you."

"What do you mean?" Pru asked. "What kind of silly game are you playing now?"

"I just bumped into you."

"So what?" demanded Pru.

"So," Freddy said, giggling a little, "I just fucked you."

"You *what?*" Pru shrieked, backing away. "You did *what?*"

But before Freddy could say another word, Pru was at the door to her room, shouting into the hall.

"Mother!" she called. "Mo–ther!"

6

Freddy's smile faded as he followed Pru to her door.

"Mo–ther!" Pru shouted again, even more loudly.

"What is it, Pru?" answered Mrs. Alexander, coming to stand at the bottom of the stairway. "For heaven's sakes!"

"Mother," Pru began to explain, still shouting, "Freddy just said the most terrible thing to me!"

"What is it?" Mrs. Alexander asked. "What terrible thing?"

"He said . . . he said," Pru started. "Ohhh, I can't just say it out loud!"

"Why ever not?" her mother wanted to know.

"I just can't!" Pru said desperately. "Not just like that."

Freddy stood behind his sister, shifting back and forth on his feet.

Mrs. Alexander put her teacup on a little table

at the foot of the stairs and started upwards. "Well," she said, taking her first steps, "you can tell me in the privacy of your room, then, if it's as bad as that."

Pru whirled around and nearly fell over Freddy. "Ohhhh!" she moaned disgustedly as she twisted past him.

"Freddy," his mother said, "perhaps you should go to your room, too. I'll be in to talk as soon as I find out what's been happening."

Freddy nodded and tried to smile hopefully up at her. His smile was only half-returned.

7

Freddy's mother stood outside his door and knocked on it, as she had taught her two children always to do.

"Who is it?" called Freddy, knowing who it was.

"It's me," answered his mother.

"O.K.," Freddy said. "You can come in."

Freddy's mother opened the door and went quickly into the room. She leaned against Freddy's desk rather than seating herself at it, and smiled at her son. "Well, Freddy," she began pleasantly.

"Yes?"

Mrs. Alexander shook her head a little and her skin turned ever-so-slightly pink. "Well," she said again.

Freddy waited.

"I guess," Mrs. Alexander said at last, "there are a few things you might like to know about."

"Like what?"

"Like the word you used with Pru just now," said his mother. "I mean, what you think you just did to her."

"Oh."

"I guess you saw the word printed some-where," said Mrs. Alexander. "Am I right?"

Freddy nodded. "At school," he said.

"Do you know what it means?"

"Bumping," said Freddy. "That's what Johnny Norman said. Bumping someone."

"Bumping," echoed his mother thoughtfully.

Freddy nodded again, "Bumping."

Mrs. Alexander took a deep breath. "Freddy," she said, "a long time ago, when you were much younger, don't you remember asking where babies came from?"

After thinking a moment, Freddy shook his head no. He wondered what that had to do with anything.

"Well," said his mother, "that's what it is."

"Making babies?" asked Freddy.

"Sometimes," answered his mother. "In a way."

Freddy thought a moment. "What other ways

are there?"

His mother laughed a little. "No other ways," she said. "I'm afraid I wasn't very clear."

Mrs. Alexander's eyes grew distant. Freddy watched her think.

"Well," Mrs. Alexander started all over again, "you've seen an electric plug, haven't you?"

"Sure I have," answered Freddy, doubtful that that had anything to do with what he needed to know.

"And you know that nothing works unless the plug is put into a socket on the wall, don't you?"

Freddy nodded, waiting for his mother to come to the point.

Mrs. Alexander smiled, brushing her hair away from her face. "Well, dear," she said, "that's what fucking is."

Freddy's eyes opened wide. "It's electric?"

His mother frowned. "What I meant was that a man . . . a man is like a plug and a woman is like a socket. When they get together, the electricity that's been waiting in the socket, or the woman, lets go and the light or the fan or the heater the plug's attached to begins to work."

"I don't understand," said Freddy simply.

"I'll try again," said his mother. She sat down at Freddy's desk and turned to face him. "Let's go back to making babies, shall we?" she said pleasantly. "Babies are stored in a woman's body, in eggs. Now, when a man's penis enters the woman, its sperm swims to an egg and fertilizes it. The baby inside begins to grow until it's large enough and ready to be born."

Freddy didn't begin to see how Johnny Norman could have been so wrong.

"Now, with electricity," his mother went on, "the socket is a storing up place for electricity. The plug at the end of the cord goes into the socket. The electricity that was waiting there meets the plug and comes out, when it's ready, lighting a bulb or a vacuum cleaner. It's quite the same thing."

"Yes," Freddy said solemnly. But he didn't understand.

"Something else, Freddy," Mrs. Alexander said. "A brother and a sister don't do this together."

"They don't?"

"No," said his mother, "because they're part of the same family."

"You and Dad are part of the same family."

"That's different," said his mother, standing up.

"We are, of course, now that we're married. But when we were children, we belonged to separate families. Your father's parents weren't mine. And mine weren't his. Our blood is different."

Blood? thought Freddy.

"You and Pru," Mrs. Alexander continued, "*are* the same. You came from the same person's eggs. Two people from the same mother and father just don't get together this way. It's not healthy."

Would he and Pru get sick? From what?

Mrs. Alexander came over to the bedside and patted Freddy's shoulder. "One last thing, dear," she said. Freddy looked up at her. "Most people don't use the word 'fuck' in their ordinary conversation. It's not considered very polite."

His mother pulled her cardigan sweater closely about her. "Now," she said, "it's bathtime. Tomorrow's Saturday. You don't want to be all tired out when you have the big game, do you?"

Freddy stood and began unbuttoning his shirt.

"Don't forget to brush your teeth and to rinse the tub when you've finished," Mrs. Alexander said. "And sleep well." She leaned down and gave the top of Freddy's head a kiss. Then she walked out of the room and down the stairs.

Later, in the bathtub, watching a model destroyer sail slowly across his body, Freddy studied himself. He sat up straighter and looked beneath the gray boat as it floated gently back and across his legs.

He knew he wasn't unusual. He'd seen other boys without clothes on. And a plug, he knew, had two prongs on it. Sometimes, he remembered, thinking of English magazines he had seen when he lived in Toronto, a plug had even three prongs.

A few minutes later, standing to dry himself, Freddy wondered about something else—what sometimes happened to him when he rubbed himself very hard with his towel. Then, without warning, his penis got longer and firmer and stronger. That must mean *something*. But his mother had mentioned nothing about it.

Freddy guessed his mother was as puzzled about everything as he was.

8

Freddy woke up cold the next morning. He had kicked his bedcovers off during the night and the temperature outside had dropped. He sleepily pulled his way to the head of the bed and parted the curtains at the window.

What he saw was the year's first snowfall. Not a very big one; not more than an inch, even, and an inch that would melt before noon. Still, it reminded him of Canada, of winds and drifts and skiing and making snow angels, of skating.

Ice skating was something Freddy truly loved. And he skated well, for he had been on ice almost as long as he had been on his feet. He knew how to use his hockey stick and how to swing around a surprised goalie. He knew how to pass the puck quickly and how to plan a play while gliding down the ice at top speed.

And yet, last year, during his last winter in

Canada, strange things had happened.

Until then, when Freddy had been knocked off his feet in action, suddenly landing on his knees or on his behind on the ice, he had always got up and skated into the fray. He hardly took enough time even to dust the snow from his trousers. But last winter, when he had been knocked down, he had rather enjoyed being down. He had liked sitting on the ice and watching for a few seconds all the color and noise around him. Twice he had lain back and just looked up at the sky above and the clouds and listened to the cutting blades.

Looking into his backyard, Freddy realized how flat the ground there was. Was it flat enough, he wondered, to build a small ice rink on? He could be the best hockey player in town if he had his own rink to practice on. All he needed were a few boards, a plastic sheet, and lots of water.

He would ask his father when he came home.

Freddy frowned. He knew what his father would say. He knew what his reasons would be. It was too solitary. It would be running away from real competition, to have your own hockey rink.

And that just wasn't fair, Freddy thought. Just as a lot of other things weren't fair. His father, for example, was what people called a "natural athlete." He could master anything he tried. He was good at everything. Including football. Freddy wasn't. And he knew it.

Freddy huddled in the bedcovers. Football. That wasn't fair, either. He was simply too small. He knew it. He felt silly just being on the field in all the equipment that was designed to make him look tough and gigantic. It almost made Freddy laugh.

But he didn't. He still had to play the game. It was a "team sport," a game where you learned to respect other people, to get along with them. Having your own ice-hockey rink was just the opposite. You wouldn't ever have to get along with anyone, unless you wanted to.

Freddy shook his head, clearing his thoughts. He looked back down into the yard and imagined his ice rink. His father would reason that Freddy didn't really need one anyway, since he already knew how to play hockey and was good at it. It wouldn't be "growing."

What would? Freddy wondered. *What would?* And then he remembered something that had caught his interest back in Toronto. It was a game played on ice, one that Freddy had never tried. If he could learn about it, master it, his father might even think he was adventurous and really interested in "team sports." Freddy tried to remember: did the game involve teams at all?

He closed his eyes. He squeezed them shut. He remembered and remembered. Yes! In his mind, he saw the same television program he had seen last year. There were lots of people on the ice, all doing something with brooms. All helping a teammate who had launched a roundish sliding object on the ice towards a target. Curling. That was the name of the game. Curling.

Freddy opened his eyes and jumped out of bed, a big smile on his face. He planned as he dressed. He would do some research. He would find out how curling was played and how its score was kept. How long the ice field had to be and how wide. How many people played. If he had a curling rink, why couldn't he, just every so often, use it to practice skating?

Freddy felt wonderful. He looked out the window again. It didn't look terribly cold. He looked at the trees lining his driveway. They did not move. There was no breeze. The early snow would melt.

The football field would be mushy, although hard enough underneath. But the topsoil would be slippery and wet. All Freddy ever had was speed. He certainly couldn't be expected to play in conditions that made him worthless to his team.

Whistling a little now, Freddy hoped that today's big game would be a game in which not everyone *did* play. Suppose the score were terribly close. No coach would take a chance on sending in a new boy. Not someone as small as he was. Certainly not.

Freddy headed down to breakfast, humming to himself, smiling as he twisted around pieces of furniture, his arm doubled up towards his chest, hugging a nonexistent football.

9

After breakfast, Freddy ambled into the small room off the living room that his mother called the library. As soon as he stepped in, he knew his research was doomed. The biggest, heaviest box of books that had been shipped south from Toronto—the one with his mother's dictionary and atlas and art books—had been misplaced during shipment. That, and one of Pru's special cartons containing her "personal" things. There was neither a dictionary in the house nor an encyclopedia.

Well, he'd just walk to the library, then. He didn't have to be in uniform and ready until two o'clock. He could walk over and nose around there a while.

Maybe, he thought, he might even find out something about that *other* subject.

Freddy went back upstairs and found his library card and a small notebook, in case there was something he wanted to write down. He took a dollar's worth of change from his top bureau drawer.

Downstairs, he bundled up and put on his boots. In the kitchen, just before leaving, he remembered to write on the blackboard where he was going. He wrote only two words: "Freddy—library."

It was only a fifteen-minute walk to the library. Freddy enjoyed the exercise, for despite the snow from the night before, it wasn't too cold. The sun was warming up, starting to melt what remained. There was hardly enough snow on the ground now to make a slush ball. Freddy was grateful for that. He was still learning about his new town. Even in Toronto, walking through unfamiliar neighborhoods in wintertime was dangerous.

"Hey, Freddy!"

Freddy turned around. Coming across the street, trailing a sled that shrieked as it scraped the pavement, was Neil Candless. His twin brother, Bruce, walked a step behind.

"Where you going?" Neil asked as he pulled even with Freddy.

"The library," Freddy answered, sloshing through a puddle.

"On a Saturday?" Neil snorted. "Boy, is that

dumb!"

Freddy smiled. Neil had freckles and was "fresh," according to Mrs. Alexander. "Not much dumber than trying to slide on this stuff," Freddy said.

"That's what *I* told him," Bruce offered.

"What else is there to do?" asked Neil impatiently.

"Go to the library," answered Freddy.

The three of them stood on a corner waiting for a light to change. Their school was directly across the street. Behind it was the hill down which Neil hoped to slide, at the same playground where the big game would be played, later.

"Why are you going there?" Bruce asked Freddy.

"To look up a couple of things," Freddy said.

"What?" Bruce asked.

"Curling," Freddy replied.

"What's that?" asked Neil.

"A kind of game."

"Oh, sure," Neil said, shaking his head as though he had known all along what curling was.

"What else?" asked Bruce. "What other things are you looking up?"

Freddy kept silent as the light changed and they crossed the street. He tried to decide whether he should say anything at all about the other subject. And should he talk about it at all? His mother had said it was a word people didn't use in ordinary conversation. That was certainly what this was. But what other word could he use?

"What other things?" Bruce prodded.

Freddy sighed. "Fucking," he said. "A book about that."

"Hooo!" Neil shouted. "I'd love to hear how you ask for a book on that!"

Freddy waited for Neil to stop laughing. He remembered Nelly's laughter the day before. Maybe, after all, fucking *was* funny. "Do you know about it?" he asked at last.

"Sure," Neil said.

"Everyone does," Bruce added.

"Oh," said Freddy.

"We found out about it years ago," Bruce said helpfully.

"You did?"

"Sure," Neil said. "What happens is this. Your peter goes into a lady and sort of feels around. Pretty soon, a baby in there grabs hold, and when your peter comes out, the baby just follows right along with it."

"Sometimes it doesn't happen right away," added Bruce. "But mostly it does."

"Oh," said Freddy.

"Everybody knows that," Neil announced. "Now you do, too."

"Any other questions," Bruce asked, smiling, "before genius here decides to slide through the mud?"

Freddy grinned and shook his head no. "Bye," he said.

Bruce grabbed Neil's collar and turned him off the sidewalk onto the grass-rimmed hill. "So long," he called, raising his hand without turning to look at Freddy.

Slopping along the sidewalk, Freddy thought about this new information. It certainly didn't match up with anything his mother had said. Nothing about eggs, anyway. Or blood.

"Geronimo!" came a distant shout.

Freddy turned and looked back. Neil's sled was creeping down the hill. Then it stopped, halfway.

Bruce, standing above his brother, bent nearly in half with laughter.

10

Freddy came to University Boulevard and turned. He was looking forward to seeing Miss Sample. She was pretty and young and he always felt she treated him somehow special. He knew she didn't, of course. Miss Sample was nice to everyone who came to the library.

The library would be on his right, with no sign hanging out front. It would just be there, standing, waiting patiently, full of books and maps and shelves —an old building that once must have been a store of some kind.

Freddy walked up to the library, automatically stretching his arm out to pull open one of its double doors. He yanked, but nothing happened. He yanked again. Still nothing moved.

Putting his hands to his face, he looked into the building. What he saw was a dark, deserted room: desks and books and magazine racks. Miss

Sample's desk and the stamps and pads on it. But he could see no people. Neither people nor movement nor light.

Freddy stepped back and looked at the doors. He had been so certain of where he was going and what he was going to do that he hadn't noticed a sign put up inside the doors. He read it now carefully, twice.

Due to a shortage of public funds, Waveland Branch Library will close to the public on November 15th. We hope you will remember the Library's other branches and, of course, the Main Library at 2nd and Locust.

Freddy thought back. The fifteenth had been only last Sunday, less than a week ago. Why hadn't Miss Sample said anything when he was there the day before that? Why hadn't she warned people? Where was she now?

Freddy stood on the sidewalk, looking at the sign and trying to decide what to do next. He didn't know where other library branches were. He did know where the main library was because his class had visited it just after the term began. But it was downtown. He would have to take a bus. Freddy had never taken a downtown bus by himself.

He looked around. Cars passed by, splashing people standing on corners. Shop windows were beginning to look Christmasy. They were dripping with tinsel and crowded with colored lights.

Freddy remembered that sometimes, when he had come to the library before, Miss Sample had had to telephone down to the main library for the particular book he wanted. If he went downtown now, he might find out more, faster, than if Waveland were open, anyway. The trip would certainly save time.

Freddy looked into the window of a jewelry shop. It was just ten. If he bussed down and back, would he be home in time for lunch and the game?

He decided to chance it.

11

Freddy got off the bus and stood on a corner, looking at the library. The building was fairly tall, four stories, and dirty gray. Its windows looked out on the city through half-pulled tan-colored shades. There was a driveway that led up a slight hill and under a portico. Huge double doors looked as though they were too heavy ever to be opened.

The library made Freddy feel smaller than ever. And nervous.

Inside, Freddy stood in the center of a large hall. The ceiling above him had windows around its edges. He craned his neck around to look at the dome above. He heard the *click-clack* of high heels and the *swoosh* of doors swinging closed.

There was no talk or laughter to be heard. But it was early in the morning yet. Freddy was among the building's first visitors.

Several cabinets stood bunched together on the

tiled floor—the card catalog, Freddy remembered. There was a check-out desk on his left and an information booth to his right. Over the doors that gave entry to the circular hall were signs: *Periodicals. Young Adults. Science and Technology.*

Freddy took a deep breath and walked towards the information booth. A woman about as old as his mother sat there, head down, reading a magazine. Freddy waited politely for her to raise her head. When, after some time, she didn't, Freddy coughed.

"Just a minute," said the woman without looking up. She turned a page quickly and scanned its reverse side. At last she looked at Freddy. "Yes?" she asked.

Freddy felt he had somehow made her angry. He smiled as warmly as he could and spoke in a very low tone of voice. "Where are the children's books, please?"

The woman's eyes went skywards. "There is a sign," she said slowly, speaking very clearly through a sigh, "just as you come in. It has a separate entrance. Downstairs." She pointed. Freddy turned to where her finger thrust.

"Outside," the woman said. "Just down a few steps, on the right."

Freddy looked back at the woman. The look on her face dared him to say anything more. "Thank you," he whispered.

He walked back across the hall and out the doors. There, to his surprise, *was* another door. Above it a signpost hung: *Children's Room. Mon.–Fri.,* 10 A.M. *to* 6 P.M. *Sat.,* 10 A.M. *to noon.*

Freddy walked down the stairway and through another set of doors into a large, very dark room which seemed filled to overflowing with shelves. There were shelves against the walls; shelves standing freely in the center of the room; shelves in closets and crannies. A few signs were scotch-taped to the walls around the room. *Our Friendly Universe. Other People, Other Lands. Danger! Picture Books.*

Freddy looked again around the room, hoping there might be someone he could say hello to, someone who might help him. He saw no one. A small desk to his left held stamps and rubber pads and notepaper and paper clips. No one sat at it.

Not wanting to waste time, Freddy walked to the card catalog. He decided it made more sense to look under C for Curling instead of S for Sports. He reached for that drawer.

Slowly, so as not to miss any one card that would help him, he thumbed his way through the cards. Where he should have found what he hoped to, he found: "Curl Up Small, Warburg, Sandol Stoddard. For further information see author card."

Freddy looked at the next card in the series but it said nothing about curling.

He decided to look under "Ice" before turning to "Warburg." He doubted Warburg's book would be what he wanted, but he would overlook nothing.

Under "Ice" he found: "Ice Hockey (as subject) see Hockey." That was that. Pressing a little farther, Freddy found other cards. "Ice Island." "Ice King." "The Ice Palace." "Ice Skating see Skating." "Ice Sports see Winter Sports."

Freddy smiled. Finally something made sense. Winter Sports ought to be in almost the same place he would look up Warburg, Sandol Stoddard. He began to feel he was getting somewhere.

He put the "Ice" tray back into its place and moved down until he came to the "Winter" drawer. He pulled it out and lifted it to the top of the cabinet. He thumbed carefully, slowly, until he came to Winter. Eagerly he turned the final card. "Winter Sports see also Hockey, Skating, Skis and Skiing, and names of other winter sports."

Freddy's smile faded. "Names of other winter sports" was where he had begun.

He put the drawer back where it belonged and stood up straight. *Well,* he thought, *there are two things I wanted to look up. I'll try the other one.*

He took a step to his left and pulled out a drawer labeled: FRUA–GARZ. He began reading. "Fuchs, Erich. Journey to the Moon." "Fuchs, Gertraut, illus. Pajaro-cu-cu; animal rhymes from many lands."

Just to check, he looked at one more card. "Fuel and Gas Dragsters," it read.

Freddy was beginning to feel just a little angry, and helpless. He wished someone would come out and offer to help him. He looked around the room again, but no one was there.

Determined to press on in spite of everything, Freddy walked to where the reference books—all the world's facts—sat on a shelf. There wasn't much point, he decided, in checking the dictionary for curling. He already knew *what* it was. What he needed to know was how it was played.

He reached out for the nearest dictionary. It was so heavy he could not hold it in his hands and thumb through it at the same time. He lifted it to the top of a cabinet and opened it, flicking to E–F.

He began at *Fucate* which, he saw, meant to rouge one's face. As an adjective it meant double-dealing. The next word, *Fuchau,* was just "(n. see Foochow)." He let his eyes wander down the page more rapidly.

Fu-civ'o-rous meant feeding on seaweed. He doubted he would have many opportunities to use *that* word. *Fucoid* was just more seaweed.

He closed the dictionary and replaced it. At least he was learning some new words as he went along. He would have that much to show for his morning.

He chose another book. "Fuchsia—a plant with handsome drooping flowers."

In the last book on the shelf, Freddy found, "Fubsy (fub'zi), adj., -si -er, -si -est. British dialect. chubby, short and fat or thick. *The manager was a fubsy man with a screwed-up signature* . . . (Punch). (*v.* fub² + -sy, as in *clumsy.*)"

Freddy closed the book with a giggle. He couldn't wait to get back to tell Johnny Norman he was a fubsy little know-it-all who didn't really know it all at all. Would he ever be mad!

"Hello," came a voice from behind him.

Freddy turned quickly, surprised, nearly dropping the book he held. He bent down and replaced
it on its shelf as quickly as he could. "Hello, ma'am,"
he said properly as he straightened.

"Have you been here long?" the woman asked.
"I'm sorry, I didn't hear anyone come in. I was back
there." She pointed to a closed door. "In my office."

"It's all right," Freddy assured her. "I was just
looking."

"For anything special?" asked the woman with
a smile. "I'm Mrs. Putnam, the children's librarian."

"Where's Miss Sample?" Freddy asked.

"Miss Sample?" Mrs. Putnam thought a moment. "Oh, yes, Miss Sample. Why, I think she's in
cataloging now."

Freddy wondered where cataloging was. "She
was nice," he said.

"Well, I hope you'll come here and enjoy using
this library now," said Mrs. Putnam. "Are you sure
you found everything you wanted? Aren't you going
to take any books home?"

Freddy shook his head. "There aren't any. Not
on what I want."

"Why, I'm sure there must be something," Mrs.
Putnam said easily. "The library is the storehouse of

almost all the information in the world. Better than that, we have no age limits, no restrictions. There's not a single book here you can't read. If you don't find a book in this department, and you have a library card —you do, of course?—yes, well, then if you can't find what you want down here, you have the entire library at your service. Somewhere I know there's a book for you."

"It's not in the catalog," said Freddy.

"Well, tell me what you want," Mrs. Putnam offered. "Maybe I can find out where your book is hiding."

Freddy looked closely at Mrs. Putnam before making up his mind. She seemed nice enough. She was even kind of pretty, with hair all gray and black like that. And she did seem to want to help.

"Now," Mrs. Putnam began, "what subjects are you interested in?"

"Curling is one," Freddy said.

"What's that?" Mrs. Putnam asked, still smiling warmly.

"It's a game you play on ice," Freddy explained. "There's probably something about it in an encyclopedia."

"Yes, that's true. There probably is. Was there

anything else?"

There was, and Freddy knew it. But how could he say so to Mrs. Putnam? His mother had warned him, but she hadn't thought to give him a different, more polite word to use for it.

"Come now, don't be shy," Mrs. Putnam urged. "You can tell me what it is."

Freddy was frantic. Here was someone who should know what he needed to know. She should know where he could go to learn about almost everything. But what could he say to her? His mother had said that people didn't use *that* word in "ordinary conversation," but she'd given him no word to use in its place.

"I'm really here just to help you," Mrs. Putnam encouraged him.

Freddy stood very straight, but his head was bent towards his shoes. "Fucking," he said, but very softly.

"What?"

He looked directly at Mrs. Putnam and raised his voice ever so slightly. "Fucking. I wanted a book about fucking."

Mrs. Putnam's face darkened and reddened and eyes watered just a little. Freddy watched.

"You mean sex education," Mrs. Putnam said quietly, after a moment.

Freddy wasn't at all sure that that was what he meant.

Mrs. Putnam turned and walked a few paces from Freddy. Freddy waited. When she turned around, Freddy saw she was smiling again.

"I'm not exactly sure what to do," she admitted.

"You mean you haven't got a book like that here?" Freddy asked.

"On sex?" Mrs. Putnam mused.

Freddy was determined there should be no misunderstanding. "On fucking," he said clearly.

"It's nearly the same thing!" Mrs. Putnam's voice rose and seemed suddenly very thin.

Freddy wondered if Mrs. Putnam knew anything at all about it. He wanted her to. But she was using so many different names. Then again, if it did have different names, that would explain the different kinds of information he had already been given.

"Are you sure it's the same?" Freddy asked. "The same as . . . as what I said?"

Mrs. Putnam breathed deeply several times and then forced a smile back onto her lips. "Of course I'm sure."

"Well, then where *do* I go to get books about it?"

"I'm rather afraid you'll have to come back again, with your mother, or with your father. The library has a policy about these things, you know. You have to have your parents' permission to take out those kinds of books."

Freddy looked at Mrs. Putnam. Then he saw something he wished he hadn't. Mrs. Putnam's face told him she had an idea. Freddy didn't know what it was going to be, but he was almost certain he wouldn't like it.

"Why don't I phone your family?" Mrs. Putnam suggested, walking quickly to the check-out desk. "If your mother says it's all right for you to have a book about sex, then I'll be glad to help you find one myself."

"I don't think so, thank you just the same," said Freddy.

Mrs. Putnam's smile changed into a smile that told Freddy he had just said what she had expected him to say. "Why not?" she asked. "Doesn't she know you're here?"

Freddy zipped up his jacket. "It's not that," he said. "She's already explained some things to me. But *she* doesn't seem very clear about it, either. Maybe I just better come back some other time."

Mrs. Putnam nodded her head, as though she were satisfied about something. "Perhaps you're right," she said. "Some other time. *With* your mother."

"Yes, ma'am," said Freddy, moving towards the doors that led out and away from the Children's Room. "Thank you anyway, though."

Mrs. Putnam stood steadfastly at her desk, her arms folded neatly and happily beneath her bosom.

Outside, as Freddy stood putting on his gloves, he heard a familiar voice call out, "Freddy? Freddy Alexander?"

He turned around and looked up. There, about to enter the library through its main doors, was Miss Sample. Freddy waved. She came down the few steps to meet him.

"Well," Miss Sample said, "you certainly are an early-morning adventurer. What did you need so desperately that you got up at dawn on a Saturday?"

"I'm always up early," Freddy confided, smiling back. "How come the library closed?"

Miss Sample's face clouded. "It's hard to explain, Freddy," she said. "Basically, we just ran out of money. We couldn't afford to run the library any more."

"That's too bad," Freddy said. "It was a nice place. Nicer than here."

"Oh, Freddy," Miss Sample said, "I hope that doesn't mean you won't visit us here just as often as you did before."

"I don't think so," Freddy said. "It's farther," he explained lamely.

Miss Sample stood up and looked seriously at Freddy, nodding her head. Freddy thought perhaps she agreed with him: a big library sometimes just wasn't as nice as a small one. In lots of ways. Then she smiled again. "Well, in case I don't see you before then, have a wonderful Christmas, Freddy."

"Happy Christmas to you, too," Freddy said. "Bye."

He turned away, and felt sad.

13

Sitting near the back of the bus with his nose pressed to the dirty glass, Freddy thought that this downtown hardly looked like a downtown as he had known it at all. Here the tallest buildings seemed tall only from a distance, and people on the streets never seemed to be dressed up. There were few shoppers— mostly women, some with children trailing out behind them as though on strings—and not much traffic.

As his bus paused at a light, Freddy puzzled at the men who stood outside a drugstore at Fifth and Grand, just stood around, nodding at each other from time to time, forgetful of the cold and wet beneath their feet.

It was so flat, this new town of his.

The bus turned northward and then quickly westward again, heading up Ingersoll, a long slow pull up a long, dull hill towards 42nd Street. A few used-car lots. Small pocket-sized shopping centers. A theater.

Freddy watched it all as though from a balcony seat. The one really different and good thing in his new town was the people he had met. In Toronto, everyone was always trying to impress you with how great their fathers were. One was in Parliament. Another owned thousands of acres in Saskatchewan. Still others owned big department stores or mines. Here everyone's father did something, but it didn't seem quite so important. You could make friends easily, without trying always to be one step ahead of the other fellow.

Of course, Freddy knew that some of his friends thought he talked a bit funny. He said "hoouse" for house, for example. And he sometimes left out words they thought should be left in a sentence—or used words his friends were unaccustomed to. "Flat" for apartment. "Lift" for elevator. And, at first, "football" for soccer.

But Freddy guessed that his differences weren't really so important as they seemed during the first few weeks of school. He did, after all, have friends. And his friends didn't tease or mimic him. He was really getting rather fond of Des Moines, although he had promised when he left Toronto that he would hate his new home.

Freddy stood up, rang the buzzer, and walked the few feet to the center doors. Waiting for the bus to slow down at 44th Street, he looked at the rubber liner around the door edges.

There, in red letters from a pen exactly like one he had on his own desk at home, was a message, bright and clear: "Fuck you!"

Freddy looked around quickly. No one looked back at him. He could remember no one getting off the bus. No one had said anything at all to anyone else during the time he had been sitting there. "Fuck you!" had probably been written on another trip.

Freddy pushed open the doors and stepped down, preoccupied. Whatever the word itself really meant, he understood now that it could mean something else. It was like "Goddamn it!" Or "Go to hell!" Or "You bastard!" Angry, unhappy, hurt.

How could someone be mad at the whole world? Freddy asked himself. For it was clear that whoever had written that had meant it for everyone, for real.

14

After lunch, Freddy stood before the mirror in his room and examined himself. He wore corduroys and gym shoes, a T-shirt, shoulder pads, and his blue-and-white jersey with the number 17 stitched on its back. His helmet lay on his bed.

He felt, and looked, silly. His shoulders seemed to stretch out for miles on either side of him. And when he put on his helmet, he suddenly became a strange sort of insect, encased protectively so that not even his eyes could be seen.

It was only a few minutes' trot to school and the playing field. Other kids would be doing the same thing: walking or bicycling or being driven by one parent or another to the scene of the game.

There was nothing he could do. No delay would be enough. It was after one-thirty. Freddy took off his helmet and went downstairs.

"Bye, Mom," he shouted into the house, not sure exactly where his mother was.

"Bye, dear," came a call. "Have fun. We'll be

cheering."

Freddy opened the door and stepped out. Only a few brownish puddles were left from the snowfall.

He took a big breath and then began to trot rhythmically down the sidewalk, turning right when he reached the end of the block and running easily towards school.

He wished his father had come back for the game. After all, it was he who had gotten Freddy into all this. The least he could do was see Freddy play a team sport.

The "Bruisers" were a group of boys who were too young to play in regulation mini-league games but who naturally wanted to play football just the same. Older brothers dubbed the team "the Baby Bruisers," but no one really minded. What mattered was the game, and the uniforms.

David Trafton, the oldest of a flock of Traftons, had organized the teams. Together with friends from college, he had set out to coach and condition the smaller children. Each team had perhaps twenty plays in its repertoire, and its members were to develop, while playing, the sense of sportsmanship and competition that their families thought important.

Freddy crossed a street and ran past Roosevelt Senior High towards his own school. He saw other players crossing the damp fields. He stood atop the hill down which Neil Candless had tried to slide earlier and looked at the field below.

There were almost forty boys in uniform. Half in blue and white, half in green and white. Freddy could see a group of parents and friends huddled along the sidelines of the chalked field. The chalk lines themselves were indistinct. The snow and its melting had made clear marking difficult.

Freddy threw himself into a slide down the hill, a careful one. He wished for just a moment that his shoes had cleats, like regular players'. But none of the Bruisers were allowed to wear them.

"Moose!" came a shout as Freddy neared the crowds.

David Trafton, bundled in a sweat suit and gloves, waved at Freddy, who waved back. "Come on, Freddy," Trafton shouted. "Warm up!"

Freddy trotted over to a group of his teammates and began bouncing up and down, shaking his arms this way and that, ducking and rising, pretending. He felt silly: not only had he never played during the season—he had never even tackled anyone except in practice. He certainly didn't feel like a football player.

The game began. Freddy's team huddled and then broke apart with a cheer. Freddy watched the offensive eleven take the field.

As the game progressed, Freddy began to realize that his wish might very well come true. The game was scoreless, a tie. Neil Candless, at quarterback, was unable to get through the other team's defense. The green-and-whites were having no better luck.

"Wow!" Johnny Norman puffed, running off the field to the sidelines as his team changed from offense to defense. "It's really messy out there!"

Freddy nodded. Half-fearing, half-hoping, he looked towards David Trafton. David made no signal, seemed not even to notice Freddy.

Half time came rapidly, and both teams retired to their own groups of fans. Freddy stood among his teammates, listening and looking, feeling useless. And just as glad, since he was, that his father hadn't come back after all.

"Freddy!" It was his mother. "Freddy, here we are!"

Mrs. Alexander, and Pru, stood atop the hill,

waving down at him. Pru was sending Freddy—long-distance—one of her special smiles.

Freddy flushed. He waved back, smiling even though he knew Pru couldn't see his smile through his helmet. Then he turned back into his group and tried to look as though he were part of the action, stamping his feet to keep out the cold and throw off the dampness that collected in his sneakers.

The second half began. During the third quarter neither team scored. It looked as though the match would be even, nothing to nothing, which would disappoint everyone.

Freddy paced the sidelines, ending up frequently behind David Trafton and Jerry Groom, his coaches. He coughed once in a while. He whistled. He clapped his hands together.

Suddenly a great shout went up from his teammates. Freddy rushed to the side of the field to see what had happened. Neil Candless had managed somehow to get the ball and his team within ten yards of the goal.

Freddy blew on his hands, clasping them together. Faster than he could follow the play, the ball got over the line. His team was out in front, six to nothing.

Johnny Norman came huffing off the field. His round little body heaved, gulping air. Johnny smiled at Freddy, who smiled back. When Johnny turned around to watch the action, Freddy let his smile fade.

The game continued. Freddy's team held its defenses. The other team had to punt. Time was running short.

Neil got his crew to the fourteen-yard line. Freddy's team and its fans were cheering, clapping, shouting for another touchdown.

The center snapped the ball to Neil, who dropped it. A loud moan went up from the sidelines. The green-and-white team had recovered.

But the cheering began to build again. Time was very short. Everyone seemed to think that Freddy's team could hold that line.

Freddy, along with the crowd, was chanting rhythmically, sending waves of encouragement out onto the field. A hand fell on his shoulder. Freddy jumped.

"Moose," David grinned down at him. "It's up to you, now, Moose. Go get 'em!"

Before he knew what had happened, Freddy had been pushed onto the field. Frantically, he looked for the boy he was to replace. He found him finally, allowing his teammate the barest chance to get off the field before the other team lined up at scrimmage for the play.

Freddy stood straight up on the grass, looking over the crouched bodies of his teammates. The ball was snapped to the other quarterback, who whirled to his right and passed it off to a halfback moving quickly behind him. The action was on the far side of the field. So Freddy stood there, watching.

"Moose!" came a cry. "Where *were* you?"

Freddy looked at Trafton, and shrugged. He crouched, just a little, as the opponents came from their huddle again.

The center hiked the ball back. The play was a confusing one. Freddy stood up to see what was happening. He didn't see the green-and-white jersey hurtling at him.

Woof! Freddy was looking up at the bright blue sky.

Slowly, a little shaken, Freddy got to his knees and then to his feet. The boy from the other team had already turned in a businesslike fashion and was trotting back towards his side.

Freddy shook his head. *What a dumb thing!* he thought. *I wasn't doing anything.*

"Get in there, Freddy!" shouted David. "Go get your man!"

Freddy didn't turn. He tried to think. Then he remembered. Even if you weren't near the play, there was still a man you were supposed to cover, someone you were supposed to "take out." He had been the player that the other boy was supposed to take out. So it had been only fair.

Freddy crouched and looked around. Bruce Candless was hunched at the ready not far away. Freddy smiled and turned "thumbs up."

The ball flew from the center's hands. The quarterback faded back to pass. Freddy was running, running harder than he had ever thought he could. Green and white flashed by him. He was aimed straight at the quarterback, who was fading to his left and was within Freddy's range.

A gun went off. A shout rose. The game was over.

Freddy slowed down, turning dejectedly towards the sidelines. Three plays. His whole season. His only game. Dumb, dumb, dumb!

He didn't look to the top of the hill. Even if Pru was sending him a special good-will smile, Freddy didn't want to have to acknowledge it.

15

Pru had gone out to a friend's house.

In the living room, Freddy's mother had set up her card table and her pencils and erasers. The week's supply of crossword puzzles, cut from the newspapers, was on her right. Her hand tapped the table furiously, her eyes were clenched shut; her mouth moved, sounding over and over a series of letters, changing one letter at a time.

Freddy liked to tease his mother about her Saturday "escapes," as she called them. All week she would purposely keep herself from even peeking at a crossword. Then, whenever the activity of a Saturday gave her time, she would set up her little office and diligently go about solving each puzzle.

Since they had left Toronto, though, his mother had been postponing her escapes each week as long as she could. With all her reference books lost somewhere between there and Des Moines, she felt unarmed, unready, and shaky.

Freddy had once tried to help her. It had been more difficult than he imagined. But since then, he had more than once looked over his mother's shoulder. He discovered words she had written in, like "khaxxx" and "xylovrite." He was sure those weren't real words. He had told her so. But each time Freddy pointed out her mistakes, his mother would turn towards him and make a falsely furious face. "Do shut up!" she would say, but rather nicely. "They fit, don't they?"

While Mrs. Alexander struggled over the past week's puzzles, Freddy and Johnny Norman were sprawled out on the floor of the little den, watching the end of a television program. After the game, Johnny had come back to Freddy's for dinner, having wheedled permission from his own family to stay until nine o'clock.

"This is awful," Johnny announced as a commercial came on. "Why do we have to watch this, anyway? There's a really good Western on channel 8."

Freddy sat up. "What do you know about Westerns?" he said. "You don't even know what fucking is."

"It was *you* who asked *me*," said Johnny. "I just told you what I knew."

"My dad always says that sometimes it takes more courage to admit you don't know something than to pretend you do."

"O.K., O.K.," Johnny answered, planting his features squarely into a show-me face. "You tell me, then, if you're so smart."

"Well," Freddy began, "I'm not exactly sure yet. But it has to do with making babies. And brothers and sisters don't do it. One of its names is sex and it has something to do with blood, too."

"Blood?" echoed Johnny.

"Blood."

Johnny's brow formed two lines between his eyes and he shook his head, thinking. "I've got it," he announced triumphantly. "I know what you mean!"

"You do?" said Freddy. "What?"

"Menstration," Johnny instructed.

"What's that?"

"That's where the blood comes in. It must be."

"What are you talking about?"

Johnny hunkered down closer to Freddy. He looked straight into Freddy's eyes. "Girls bleed," he said in a half-whisper.

"They do?"

"Yep."

"Where?"

Johnny paused. "Their tits," he said.

"What?"

Johnny nodded as though Freddy all along had known and agreed with him. He was very serious. "Once a month," he said, "blood comes out."

"I never knew that," Freddy admitted.

"Well," Johnny mused, "maybe Pru isn't doing it yet. But *my* sisters are. Both of them."

"How do you know?" asked Freddy. "Have you ever seen it?"

Johnny shook his head no. "But I will," he said firmly.

"That must be terrible," Freddy said.

"Every one of them does it, though," Johnny answered. "Haven't you ever heard of Kotex?"

"What's that?" asked Freddy.

"A sort of bandage. Girls stick it in their bras, to keep the blood from leaking out."

"Are you sure?"

"Of course I'm sure!" Johnny was beginning to lose patience. "You think I'd go around making these things up?"

Freddy thought this over for a moment. "I guess not," he said. "I just don't get it."

"There's nothing to get," Johnny said sharply. "It's just something every girl does. Until they get old. Then they have a menstral pause."

"It stops, just like that?"

"Yep."

The two boys knelt on the floor, looking at each other. Johnny couldn't think of anything more to add. Freddy didn't know what questions he should ask. The information was so new, so astonishing. He wondered about Pru. Maybe he should try to see if she was bleeding, too.

"This show is terrible," said Johnny, standing up and stretching. "I'm going home. I can watch what I want to there!"

Freddy sat on the floor, unmoving, still thinking.

"See you tomorrow?" asked Johnny, putting on his coat.

Freddy looked up at Johnny a minute and then remembered something he had learned. "Sure, Fubsy," he said.

"What was that?"

"I said, see you tomorrow, Fubsy." Freddy's smile became a chuckle.

"What's *that* supposed to mean?" Johnny wanted to know. "What does that mean, anyway?"

"Look it up, Fubsy," said Freddy. "You know everything!"

"Probably some dumb Canadian thing!" snorted Johnny, turning and walking out of the room.

16

Freddy's mother turned out his light and went down-stairs. Not quite sleepy yet, Freddy pulled himself to the top of his bed. He parted the curtains and looked out into the yard. Snow was falling again. This time, Freddy thought, it might be a real snow, a big one.

He smiled. With snow on the ground, tomor-row's skating party would be more what it should be. A hot-chocolate skate-in. All the Bruisers and their coaches and friends would be there.

Freddy crossed his arms along the window sill and let his head rest on them. Staring out at the floating whiteness, he felt warm and safe in bed. But not sleepy. He was thinking about Johnny Nor-man's bleeding sisters.

Freddy sat up in bed. He threw his legs over its edge. He would stay up until Pru came home. Then, ever so carefully, sneaking out of his own room to hers, he would look through her keyhole. Suppose she were bleeding. Surely it would show as she undressed. It would have to show *somewhere*.

Freddy pulled back his covers and sat there, swinging his legs, getting a little chilly. He would not allow himself to try to stay awake in bed, warm and comfortable. Too often, as on a New Year's Eve, he had made a resolution to stay awake. But then, in bed, he would fall asleep anyway, simply because he *was* warm and comfortable. Not this time.

He sat on his bed and hummed a little, very softly. It was not too long before he heard the front door slam and heard the voices of his mother and his sister downstairs. He slipped off the bed and crept to the door, putting his ear to it.

Pru was coming up the stairway slowly. His mother called something to her Freddy couldn't quite make out. Pru replied, "O.K., Mom, I will. 'Night."

Freddy waited until he heard Pru's footsteps pass his door and approach her own. He heard the *click* of her door being shut.

Stealthily Freddy opened his door. He looked out, checking both ways. He closed the door behind him, leaving it open just a little should he have to duck back inside suddenly.

On tiptoe he approached Pru's door. He could hear nothing, either from her room or from downstairs. He knelt on the carpet and put his eye to the keyhole.

Pru was sitting on her bed, still wearing her coat. She gave a huge, sudden sigh and bent down to slip off her shoes. With another sigh, she threw herself backwards, sprawling on the bed without undressing.

Freddy waited. Pru didn't move. Maybe she was so tired she was going to sleep fully clothed. Freddy felt cheated.

Then Pru sat up. Freddy's breath shortened. She stood up and walked away from the bed. Freddy couldn't see her.

Before Freddy knew what was happening, he saw Pru coming slowly towards the doorway, her make-up kit in hand, on her way to the bathroom. Freddy hadn't time even to stand up. He scurried down the hall on his hands and knees and ducked back into his own room.

Pru opened her door. She stood in the hallway, just outside her room. Freddy's heart seemed to stop. Then he peeked out from his doorway.

Pru stood in the hall, her kit in hand, staring at him. "Hmmph!" she said, seeing his head poke around the doorjamb. Then she turned and walked quickly down the hall.

Freddy shut his door. He went to his desk and picked up his alarm clock. Painstakingly, he set it for a time when Pru would not yet have awakened.

17

The alarm went off. Freddy jumped out of bed and darted across his room. He pushed the alarm button back in and stretched. Outside, the sun was shining, but not very strongly. It was still early.

He went to the window and looked down into the backyard. The snow had stopped during the night, but the fall had been heavy enough, and the wind quick enough, so that in some places very high and very inviting drifts were just waiting for someone to plunge into them. Freddy smiled happily and put on his bathrobe.

Quietly he opened his door. There were no sounds in the house. His mother and Pru were still asleep. As they were supposed to be, according to Freddy's plan. He eased his way down the hall towards his sister's room and knelt before her door. He looked through the keyhole.

Pru was just turning in her bed. A hand seemed

to fly out of the covers and then fall back into another position, hidden, more comfortable. Freddy waited. And waited.

Finally, Pru sat up, her eyes still closed. As though opening them were the most dangerous thing in the world to do, Pru opened first one eye and then the other warily. She threw back her covers and dashed across the room for her bathrobe, too quickly for Freddy to see anything. Once it was on, over her nightgown, she seemed to feel better.

Pru disappeared from the line of Freddy's vision for a moment. When she moved back into it, she was carrying a magazine. She walked to her bureau and spread it out on top, turning to a particular page. She stood before her mirror, scanning the magazine, nodding a little.

Pru stepped back from the bureau and spread her arms wide at shoulder level. Then, Freddy saw, she pushed her arms back even farther, very slowly, and very slowly she brought them together in front of her body.

She breathed in, loudly, as her arms again were stretched at shoulder level to reach behind her. Freddy heard Pru exhale as she brought them forward again.

On his knees, Freddy wondered what on earth Pru was doing. Exercises of some kind. But what were they for? He shifted on his knees and continued to watch, still hopeful.

After a dozen repetitions of her exercise, Pru stopped. Again she moved out of Freddy's range of vision. When she returned, she had taken off her nightgown although she still wore her robe. She turned sideways to the mirror and pulled the robe tight against her body. She seemed to be looking at her breasts.

Freddy strained to see if any stains were on her robe. He saw none. Maybe the exercising was to get the blood flowing, he decided. He waited.

Pru bent over a little and put her hands together in front of her body. She laced her fingers and then seemed to squeeze her elbows in towards her body very, very slowly. She let her arms relax and stood straight again. Once more she bent over, after breathing a moment, and pushed her arms until her forearms met. Erect again, she breathed deeply.

Freddy was baffled. If she were trying to get her blood flowing, why didn't she just hit herself, or squeeze something?

After a few more minutes of exercising, Pru

stopped and turned to the mirror. She pulled her flannel robe close about her and looked into the glass. Whatever she saw seemed to please her, for she smiled at herself in the mirror.

Pru stepped a pace away from her reflection and formed her features into an odd-looking expression. Freddy couldn't be certain what kind of face Pru thought she was making. To him, it just looked funny. Pru's half-smile was reflected for Freddy to see, and her eyes were only half opened. She had wet her lips with her tongue until they glistened.

For almost a minute she stood looking at herself. Then she changed her pose and opened her robe.

This is it! Freddy thought. *At last!*

But because of the angle from the keyhole to the mirror, all he could see was Pru's face in the glass. The rest of her body was below his line of sight. Freddy was disappointed. But he waited nonetheless, hoping Pru would turn his way while her robe was still wide open.

She didn't. Instead, she closed her robe and drew its belt around her waist. She still stood before the mirror. With her hands, Pru maneuvered the robe around until its neckline and the break in it, all the way down to the floor, were slightly off center. The robe was still tied, but only just, so that a line of skin from her feet to her throat was visible. Again Pru half-closed her eyes and wet her lips. She turned a little.

Freddy could see part of Pru's entire leg now, from her bare foot all the way up past her hip. Silently he pleaded with her to stop all the fooling around and let him see what he wanted. But Pru stood admiring herself and her long, beautiful leg, and seemed to have no intention of showing Freddy anything else. After all, Freddy realized, she didn't even know he was there.

Pru tousled her hair a little, until most of it seemed to fall into her eyes. She preened, turning one way and then another. She put a hand to the top of her robe and parted it just a little more. Freddy could see her neck and the top of her chest.

Then, abruptly, Pru disappeared from where Freddy could see. He waited.

The door opened so quickly Freddy hadn't even time to change his posture. Towel in hand, Pru looked down at her brother, her mouth beginning to open.

"Sex fiend!" she screamed. "Mo—ther!"

She slammed the door in Freddy's face.

Caught, Freddy wasn't sure what to do. Running back to his room would gain him nothing. The damage had been done. If he waited right there, on hands and knees, and kept watching, he might still see something.

Inside her room, Pru paced back and forth, swinging her arms in fury. Freddy could hear her talking to herself. "My own brother," Pru said to no one in particular. "My own brother! Ohhh!"

Again the door was pulled open and Pru confronted Freddy.

"I hope you got an eyeful," she screamed at him. "You—you—sex maniac!"

Freddy stood up. Then he ducked, for Pru had swung at him.

"Mo–ther!" Pru cried again. "Mo–ther!"

Freddy smiled a little at his sister. "Take it easy," he tried. "I was only—"

"Don't even speak to me!" Pru cut him off, still raging.

"Why, Pru," Mrs. Alexander said, coming out of her bedroom into the hall, still fastening her robe. "*What* is going on?"

"Mother," Pru half whined, half shouted,

"Freddy is a Peeping Tom! My own brother, spying on me! You have to make him stop! Honestly!"

"Freddy?" his mother questioned.

Freddy's ears reddened. "I was only—"

"Yes?" his mother urged.

"I wanted to see the blood," Freddy admitted.

"Eeeee!" Pru screamed. She stepped back into her room and slammed the door.

18

Mrs. Alexander stood in the hallway without moving. Freddy waited, wondering whether he was going to be punished.

"I guess, Freddy," his mother said slowly, "that I didn't answer your questions as well as I had hoped."

Freddy said nothing. His mother put a hand on Freddy's shoulder and gently guided him back into his room.

"It sounds," said Mrs. Alexander, closing his door after them, "as if you've heard something about menstruation."

"That's what Johnny calls it," said Freddy, relieved to find that he and his mother and Johnny were all talking about the same thing.

His mother nodded. She and Freddy sat on his unmade bed, facing each other. "All right," said Mrs. Alexander. "I'll try to explain what Johnny perhaps couldn't."

Mrs. Alexander twisted just a bit more, hitching one leg up underneath her on the bed and wrapping her robe modestly around herself.

"Now," she said, "when a girl grows into a woman, certain changes take place in her body. At a certain time, and it isn't always the same time for every girl, her body begins to tell her that she is old enough to have a baby."

"How?" asked Freddy. "How does it tell her?"

Freddy's mother smiled. "What happens, Fred, is that the wall that lines her uterus—the big space inside her where a baby would grow—builds up vitamins and chemicals and food for a baby. If no sperm enter the girl to fertilize the egg, the uterus washes itself out after a while and starts all over again."

"I don't get it," Freddy said simply.

"Well," said his mother, "try it this way. A woman's body has to feed a baby before it's born. Part of that food is built up and stored in her body. If a baby doesn't get started right away, the food goes to waste. So, as in an old-fashioned refrigerator, the body needs to be defrosted, cleaned. And that's what happens. All the vitamins and chemicals and food come out. They come out through the vagina of a woman, the same place a man's penis would enter the woman to put his sperm. That's what's called bleeding, or menstruation. It takes about a month for the food to build up each time, and a few days for it to be washed out."

"But what about Pru?" insisted Freddy. "Is she doing it?"

"Well, Freddy," said his mother, "if you must know, yes. But it really isn't anyone's concern except her own. I wouldn't talk about it with her, if I were you."

Freddy nodded.

His mother stood up and walked to the door. "You seem to have so many questions," she said. "Perhaps, when your father gets back, you and he can have a longer talk about all this." Mrs. Alexander smiled at Freddy then, a nice smile.

"One little thing more," said Freddy's mother quickly. "I think it might be a good idea if, just for the morning, you stayed out of Pru's way."

"O.K., Mom," Freddy said. "That's fine with me."

And it was. Even though he had ducked once this morning, Pru was fast. Freddy couldn't hope to avoid her hand successfully all day long.

Besides, he thought, if Pru was doing it, then she was almost—no, she *was*—a woman. A man wasn't supposed to hit a woman back, ever. A boy might once in a while get one off at his sister, but what if his sister was a woman old enough to have babies?

19

The snow that had fallen the night before was deep
enough and wet enough to do almost anything with:
make snowmen, make snow angels, build a fort.
Freddy ran along the sidewalk, kicking up snow
spray, followed by Pru and his mother. He was
happy to be out of church at last, free again to do
what he felt like doing, ready for lunch and the hike
to Greenwood Pond for the party.

He turned into his driveway and then, suddenly, almost losing his balance, he stopped. There
were car tracks in front of him.

"Dad!" he shouted, beginning to run alongside the house, following the tracks. He was about
to stop and turn and go into the house through a
side door when he heard hammering. He looked
around, and then back towards the garage.

His father stood on a ladder, bundled against
the chill and wearing gloves. He was nailing a big,

flat white board with a ring attached to it above the garage doors.

"Dad!" Freddy shouted again, running towards him.

Mr. Alexander turned around and jumped down from the ladder.

"Why, Frederick Powell Alexander the First!" said his father, laughing, bending down to lift Freddy off his feet. He tossed Freddy into the air and then dropped him into a snowbank on the edge of the drive. Freddy grinned up at his father. "Did you bring me anything?" he asked.

"Have I ever not brought you something?" countered Mr. Alexander, as he stepped back onto the ladder and moved upwards.

"What is it?" Freddy asked. "What?"

"This," said his father.

"That?"

"It's a backboard," explained his father.

Freddy's face went blank. "For basketball," added Mr. Alexander.

"Oh," said Freddy.

Mr. Alexander pounded away a moment. Then he spoke over his shoulder. "Fred," he said, "why don't you go get a broom and sweep some of this snow away? You can't dribble a basketball on snow, you know."

"But, Dad," said Freddy, "how can I play hockey and basketball at the same time?"

"You can't, of course," said his father reasonably, climbing off the ladder and looking up at his handiwork. "But I wouldn't be at all surprised if, after just fooling around here for a while, you didn't decide that basketball was a lot more fun than hockey any old day."

Freddy didn't say so, but he thought that *he* would be surprised if that happened.

Mr. Alexander clapped his hands together and started to walk back towards the house. Freddy walked alongside him.

"The ball's inside," said Mr. Alexander. "After lunch, when you've cleared the court, we'll toss it around together."

Freddy nodded, remembering the skating party but saying nothing. He stood outside the doorway as his father walked into the house and then returned, handing Freddy a broom.

Freddy turned around and walked back towards the garage.

He didn't want to sweep the cement. He didn't

want to play basketball. As far as he knew, you had to be seven feet tall to be any good at it. Looking ahead, Freddy doubted he would ever be seven feet tall.

But how could he tell his father all this? He didn't want to seem ungrateful. But why was basketball better than hockey? Both used teams. Both were popular in the United States. It wasn't as though playing hockey was running away from anything.

Standing beneath the basket, Freddy shrugged and took a half-hearted swipe at the snow around him. He tried always to be what his father wanted. But it wasn't fair for Freddy to have to be his father's *son*, unless Mr. Alexander wanted to be his son's *father* just as much.

Do all fathers do this? Freddy asked himself. Did they all take one look at the baby, see it was a boy, and begin planning? Would he do that if he were a father?

But suppose I didn't want to play anything, thought Freddy. Not basketball or football or even hockey. Suppose I just wanted to be a genius. Would that be enough for him? For anyone's father?

Freddy took another swing at the snow, and then a third, beginning now to work in a path. It wasn't as easy as it looked. The tracks from his father's car had packed the new snow down. A broom simply couldn't get it all up. He would have to get a shovel. He laid down the broom and walked slowly towards his house.

What he saw as he entered the kitchen was his parents, sitting at the small table, holding hands. And kissing very gently across the table. Freddy smiled. "Excuse me," he said.

His mother blushed. "Hey, Fred," called his father. "I guess your mother still hasn't managed to teach you to knock, eh?"

"When I come into the kitchen?" Freddy asked with a laugh.

His father laughed, too. "I guess you're right," he said, standing up. "Tell you what, Fred. Take off your things and go into the library. I'll be there in a minute. We can have a little catching-up session, just the two of us."

"O.K.," said Freddy, kicking off his boots at the kitchen door. Mr. Alexander walked from the kitchen into the dining room as his wife smiled to herself and turned away to finish preparing lunch.

In the hall, Freddy took off his jacket and gloves and went to find his father. Mr. Alexander was seated in the small den, in a corner, with paper and pencil in hand. "Hi," he said. "Come on in."

Freddy walked in and sat on the carpet at his father's feet, crossing his legs and sitting like an expectant Buddha.

"Well, Fred," started his father, "how've you been?"

"O.K.," said Freddy.

"Everything going well at school?"

"Pretty much."

"I'm sorry I wasn't here yesterday. How'd it go?"

"O.K.," Freddy said, hoping he wouldn't have to say much more. "We won."

Mr. Alexander paused. Freddy waited, looking at him.

"Well, Fred," Mr. Alexander said again. "Your mother tells me you're interested in how people sleep together."

"I am?"

"Maybe that's the wrong phrase. Sex, I mean," said his father.

Freddy remembered. "That's the same thing as fucking," he said, wanting to know that he and his father were talking about the same thing.

His father smiled a little. "I guess you could say that."

Freddy smiled back at his father. *He* hadn't been disturbed about Freddy's saying the word out loud.

Then Freddy wondered what sleeping together had to do with anything. No one had mentioned *that* to him before.

20

Freddy looked expectantly at his father, who was busy looking back down at him. Mr. Alexander had a smile on his face. He coughed once, and cleared his throat. "I'll be as plain about this, Fred, as I can. You ask any questions that come into your head."

"O.K.," agreed Freddy.

At the end of a sigh, Freddy's father began. "First of all, fucking is something most people do. It's not mysterious. It's not anything dirty. And it has a lot of names."

Freddy had expected that.

"Sleeping together," his father went on, "is what some people call it. What fucking is, Fred, is when two people, a man and a woman, are physically united. Sexual intercourse, another name for it, takes place then."

"How?" asked Freddy.

"Well, mostly it happens in bed."

"Why?"

"Let's back off a ways, shall we, just to learn a little more about it?"

Freddy waited.

"Now," began his father all over again, "you know how boys are made. And you know how girls are made. A boy has a penis and testicles. A girl has a vagina. It is an opening that was made just for the penis. God's blueprints are very exact."

Freddy's father nodded to himself as though pleased about what he had said. "God made it so that two people could get together and have sex and produce children easily. The woman's vagina is about where your penis and testicles are."

Mr. Alexander began drawing something on the pad he held on his lap, but he didn't show it to Freddy. "All right," he said, "now let's go on."

"O.K."

"Fucking, Fred, is simply the act of two people joining. The man's penis enters the woman's vagina." Mr. Alexander stopped and looked expectantly at his son. Freddy had no questions to ask.

Mr. Alexander pressed on. "After a while, a sort of juice comes out of the man's penis, called semen. In it are sperm, millions of them. In order for a baby to begin to grow, one tiny sperm from the man has to enter an egg inside the woman's uterus."

Again Mr. Alexander stopped and waited.

"Mom told me about that, the uterus," said Freddy.

Mr. Alexander nodded, but he also frowned a little. "Right," he said. "Now on either side of the uterus, in the ovaries, are—"

"What's that?" asked Freddy.

Mr. Alexander's face brightened. "The ovaries," he explained, "are where human eggs are stored. Hundreds and hundreds of them. Very small. So small you can hardly see one without a microscope. Usually, Fred, only one egg comes out of the ovaries at a time. The sperm that come from a man's penis have to penetrate that egg. Only one sperm has to get into it. When this happens, the egg is fertilized."

Mr. Alexander stopped expectantly again. When Freddy said nothing, he asked, "Your mother tell you about fertilizing?"

Freddy nodded.

"All right," said Freddy's father, sounding a little brusque. "After the egg is fertilized, it begins a new life of its own, growing inside the woman's body. As the fetus grows—"

"The what?"

"That's what the baby is called, before it's fully grown—a fetus," explained Mr. Alexander, his voice a little softer and slower again. "As it grows, the woman's uterus expands. Like a balloon when you push air into it. That's what you see when you see a pregnant lady. Her uterus has grown in order to let the fetus inside grow until it's ready to come out as a full-grown baby."

Mr. Alexander paused, scribbled something on his pad, and smiled a little to himself. Freddy wondered if he were finished.

21

When his father said nothing more, Freddy coughed. "Is it fun?" he asked.

"What?"

"Sex."

Mr. Alexander cleared his throat. "Yes, it is," he said.

"Why?"

Freddy's father scribbled again on his pad. Maybe, thought Freddy, his father was only doodling.

"Because it gives pleasure to both the man and the woman," said his father.

"How?"

"Well, Fred," his father said and then stopped. His brow crinkled a little. "Certain parts of our bodies, when touched in the right way, sort of make us tingle. A woman has a small organ near the opening to her vagina called a clitoris. When a man touches that, it makes her tingle. For a man, just having his penis in a woman's vagina is exciting."

"Oh," said Freddy. It didn't sound that exciting to him. Tingling was what he did when he heard "God Save the Queen." Or when he used to, in Canada.

"There's one other thing, Fred," Mr. Alexander said. "Fucking doesn't always mean a baby will be born."

"Why not?"

"Well, because. Sometimes no sperm ever reaches an egg. And sometimes people just don't want to have babies. There are pills a woman can take so that she won't have one. Sometimes people like to have sex just for the fun of it."

Freddy heard, but he was already thinking of something else. "Is 'fuck' a bad word?" he asked.

"Not necessarily," Mr. Alexander said. "Except that people use it the wrong way. They use it when they're angry or when they want to hurt someone else's feelings. It really isn't polite, Fred. I guess that's what it is. It's used too frequently when really some other word fits a thought much better."

Freddy nodded. He was getting hungry. He wanted to ask about building an ice rink of his own.

He wanted to—

"Let's see," said his father, sitting back in his chair, his hands on its arms. "Is there anything else?"

Freddy hoped not.

With pencil and pad still in his lap, Mr. Alexander seemed to be tracing back over what he had said, everything in order. "I know," he announced, leaning forward again. "I forgot something."

"What?" asked Freddy, hoping whatever it was would be short.

"We know how a girl understands she's ready to have babies. But we haven't mentioned how a boy knows he's ready to provide the sperm."

"How does he?"

"Well" said his father, "boys become young men at different ages. Sometimes at twelve. Sometimes at thirteen or fourteen. In any case, you'll know when the time comes."

"But how?" asked Freddy. "How?" This might be really important.

"The usual way," explained his father, "is that one night you'll have a dream. You may not even remember what it is about. But when you wake up the next morning—or if you wake in the middle of the dream itself—you'll find that your bed is damp, wet from the semen that your penis has sent out."

"What kind of dreams could I have?" asked Freddy.

His father chuckled a little. "Well, they could be about almost anything. But probably they'll have to do with young ladies. Beautiful ones. When it happens, Fred, you'll know, so there's no need to be alarmed by it or ashamed of its happening. With sex, everybody has more or less the same problems and the same ideas."

"What was your dream about?" asked Freddy. "The one you had that told you you were ready?"

"I don't remember, Fred," said his father. "Perhaps I should, but I don't. I do remember, though, getting up that morning, afterwards, and waking up your Uncle Fred to tell him about it."

"What did he say?"

"Not much. He was already old enough to have had the same thing happen to him. He wasn't very helpful."

"Did you fuck a girl right away?" asked Freddy.

His father laughed outright. "Oh my, no!" he said. "It was many years before I got round to doing that."

"But what about your sperm?" asked Freddy. "Didn't it go bad? Doesn't it have to defrost?"

"Well," said his father, leaning back and looking at Freddy in a way that made Freddy feel he had asked a question that pleased his father. "In a way. What we call 'wet dreams' take care of that."

"But when did you, finally, fuck?" Freddy wanted to know.

His father smiled rather softly then. "I guess I was old-fashioned, Fred. I waited until I met your mother. She was, and is, the woman I fell in love with."

"You must have done an awful lot of dreaming," Freddy decided.

Mr. Alexander laughed again. "I did. Fred," he said. "Believe me, I did."

"But you don't have to be married, do you, to do it." Freddy mused.

"Well, Fred, it isn't necessary to be married to have intercourse. But it certainly helps if you like the young woman."

"Oh," said Freddy.

"And it's nicer if she likes you, too."

Freddy thought he could understand that. Then

he remembered something. Why, when he was rubbing himself down after his bath, did his penis sometimes stiffen and stretch out? Was that how . . . ?

"Hey, you two men, lunch!" called his mother from another room.

Freddy jumped up very quickly, and put his hands on top of his father's arms. There wasn't enough time for *that* question, Freddy decided. There was something on his mind far more important.

Mr. Alexander could have stood up if he'd wanted to, but he seemed to sense there was something urgent in his son's serious face. Something that hadn't to do with sex at all.

22

Freddy's father sat back and waited, patiently. Freddy felt very hot. He coughed. He looked at his father. He took a step backwards.

"I don't want to play basketball," Freddy announced. His voice was very low but his father could hear him easily. "And I don't want to play football next year, either."

Mr. Alexander did not smile. He looked at Freddy. Then, speaking gently, he said, "But Freddy, yesterday's game must have been pretty good. Your team won."

"I don't care," Freddy said. "I'm too small. I didn't help. I want to do things I'm good at."

"But how do you know you won't be good at basketball?" his father asked patiently. "You haven't given it a try yet."

"You have to be tall to play it," said Freddy.

Mr. Alexander smiled at last. "That's just not so, Fred," he said. "There are some terrific players who aren't giants."

"But I can be good at my own things," Freddy insisted. "I can play hockey. I can run. When I grow up I can find other things, too."

Mr. Alexander stood up at last. "Are you mad at me, Fred?" he asked. "Because I couldn't come back in time for yesterday?"

Freddy looked at his father without blinking. "I was," he admitted, "a little. But I'm not now."

"And you won't even try with basketball?"

Freddy hesitated. Trying, he knew, wasn't such a big thing. "Well," he said, thinking it over, "I could try. But it's me who gets to decide things. If I like it, O.K. But if I don't, then I get to stop. I just want things to fit me." Freddy shook his head determinedly. He spoke even more quietly. "It would be nice if maybe you could do some things with me."

Mr. Alexander opened his mouth to speak, but Freddy went on in a rush. "I don't mean you should quit work or anything. But maybe, every so often, you could be around a little more."

"Just for fun?" asked his father with a smile.

"Yes," said Freddy. "Just for fun. We could do things."

"Hey, fellows!" called Mrs. Alexander. "Freddy, you'll miss your skating party."

Suddenly, Mr. Alexander bent down and

grabbed Freddy's legs. With one motion, he up-
ended Freddy and threatened to drop him head first
to the floor. Freddy let out a hoot of delight, knowing his father wouldn't really let go.

Then together they walked into the dining
room.

Pru was already seated. Mrs. Alexander was
carrying in a platter of chicken. The mashed potatoes
and peas were already on the table, as were the salad
and wine.

Freddy sat down opposite his sister while his
father walked into the kitchen to see if there was
anything he could do to help.

Pru glowered at Freddy a moment, and then
snapped her head away and would not look again
at him. Through her teeth she muttered, "I hope
you're happy, Tweenie. Now you know it all."

Freddy blushed. He didn't see what it had to do
with Pru, anyway. Then Pru giggled. "A lot of good
it will do you," she said. "Midgets never do it!"

Freddy looked both ways before he formed the
words with his lips. It wasn't polite. But no one ever
said he couldn't just pretend to say it.

"Dad—dy!" screamed Pru, wheeling in her
chair. "Dad—dy!"

23

During lunch, Mr. Alexander sneaked looks at the boy on his right. He shook his head once, silently. Twice he smiled. And he winked across the table at his wife more than once.

Freddy wasn't certain what his father was thinking. But he didn't think it could be anything bad. It seemed to him that his father was pleased about something. Almost proud. But of what precisely, Freddy wasn't certain.

Nonetheless, without knowing why exactly he felt this way, Freddy was almost sure he could have his own skating rink, if he asked for it.

He looked down at his plate and played a little with his vegetables. Suddenly he thought of Johnny Norman. Wait till I tell him, Freddy thought. Wait till he finds out how much he doesn't know!

Then Freddy remembered the question he had been about to ask when his mother had called,

"Lunch!" It had something to do with his bath, with what sometimes happened when he toweled himself dry.

Was that how a man's penis got in in the first place? It must be. It just had to be. Otherwise, how—?

Freddy looked up at his father. His father smiled at him.

Freddy knew suddenly he couldn't ask his father about it. Not here, not with Pru and his mother around. And not for a while, anyway. To ask one more question now, any question, when his father was feeling so sure he had answered everything perfectly, just might hurt his feelings.

Freddy smiled back at his father.

24

With their skates slung over their shoulders, the two boys reached Polk Boulevard and turned south towards the park. Freddy thought he could already hear the shouts and cries and laughs of people on the ice.

Sloshing through snowbanks and slipping along frozen patches, Freddy felt older and taller and very much smarter than Johnny. He knew about bleeding and babies and sex. He was on fire to show off, but he had to pick the right moment.

The problem was, how to go about getting the most out of his new information. He might casually utter the word "menstruation" at Johnny, accenting the second syllable—the syllable that Johnny didn't seem to know existed at all.

They crossed Grand Avenue and cut through a corner of the Art Center's lawn.

The trouble was, suppose Johnny knew about

the bathtub thing. Suppose he knew and would laugh at Freddy for not knowing. Freddy was almost certain he had everything figured out, but he was only *almost* certain.

Johnny ran on ahead of Freddy, towards a happy noise. Freddy could see the ice through the bare black trees.

He followed, walking, thinking. What he needed was someone besides his father he could ask. He just had to be surer than sure before he said anything to Johnny. He had to be. But who?

"Come on, Freddy!" shouted Johnny over his shoulder. "Come on!"

25

In spite of the slight thaw the day before, Saturday night's big snow and dropping temperatures had kept Greenwood skatable. It was too early in the season for the warming house to be open, but Tina and a few of her friends had set up two card tables on the edge of the ice, with milk cans and thermos jugs full of hot chocolate on top of them. Brownies were spread out in cardboard boxes alongside.

The pond was a whirling mixture of color and shouting. David Trafton and Jerry Groom swept around the rink, tagging skaters with a slap on the behind or a knock on the head. Behind them skated a mob of boys in pursuit.

"Fubsy" Norman, huffing and puffing a bit to keep up with Freddy, fell on his knees as his momentum outreached his balance. Freddy skidded to a stop to laugh, skate back, and help him up.

"Aw, Fubsy," Freddy teased. "Maybe skating

just isn't for you. Fubsy people don't have what it takes, sometimes."

Johnny pulled himself up and stood on the ice, nervous but undeterred. "I don't think that's funny," he said. "Not funny at all. My mother says I'm fubsy because of my glands. Besides, you shouldn't make fun of something a person can't help."

Freddy heard his own voice saying exactly the same thing to Pru, but he couldn't help himself. "My aunt is always saying she has bad glands, too," he told Johnny. Then he laughed. "But my dad says she just loves to eat!"

Freddy dug his skates into the ice, jumping out of reach of Johnny's swinging arm. He skated away, crouched in speed, with Johnny lumbering after him, determined to catch Freddy but uncertain of his skill.

Freddy heard the wind in his ears. He opened his mouth. He liked feeling the cold on his teeth.

Going as fast as he was, suddenly Freddy found himself gliding across the ice even faster. David Trafton had cut between him and Johnny, bent down, and given Freddy a huge push from behind.

Freddy turned to see what had happened, and saw David grinning at him.

That was it! David would know! He would know whether getting stretched out and stiff meant anything, meant what Freddy thought it meant. He could ask David.

"Hey, David!" Freddy called. "Wait!"

Freddy dragged his right skate, slowing down as David turned his head at his call.

Johnny smashed into him, from behind. Freddy sailed forward through the air, landing hard on his chin.

After they had untangled themselves and were sitting facing each other, only Johnny seemed to be aware of where he was. "You dummy!" he said, crawling to his knees and standing shakily. Freddy sat on the ice, not moving.

"Hey," said Johnny, bending down to get a close look at Freddy's face. "You're bleeding."

Freddy put a glove to his chin. But he didn't bother to take it away to see whether or not he really was bleeding.

He was trying to picture two people in bed, lying down. First he pictured them side by side, facing one another. Then he thought perhaps the man would have to be on top of the woman, in order to have his penis fall into her vagina. Otherwise, it made no sense. Side by side, he couldn't imagine that a penis just crawled inside by itself. Like a worm. Gravity was the only answer he could think of. If a man lay on top of a woman (but wasn't he too heavy?), his penis would just naturally hang down and fall in. Sort of. Unless, of course, the man had been rubbing himself with a towel. Then it wouldn't have to only fall in. It would fit in.

"Hey, Moose! You all right?" David Trafton was standing nearby, looking down at Freddy still sitting on the ice.

Johnny pointed at Freddy's chin and David slid over a few feet more. "Oops!" said David. "That's quite a cut."

Freddy stood up, David's arm steadying him. The cut didn't hurt, but blood was running down his chin, and his neck.

"Come on, Moose," David Trafton said, guiding Freddy across the ice. "I've got a first-aid kit in my car. We'd better patch you up." Johnny Norman, left alone, shrugged and turned away, precariously starting on his own across the pond.

"Hospital call!" David shouted at Tina as they neared the card table. Tina's forehead creased quickly, and her eyes sent a wave of sympathy to

Freddy. Freddy doubted it was as serious as all that.

"Here, fellows," said Tina, walking over with two mugs full of hot chocolate. "A tranquilizer to steady the surgeon's hand, and an anesthetic for the patient."

"Thanks, love," said David. He took both mugs and placed them on the stone embankment that ran around the pond. Then, easily, with his hands beneath Freddy's arms, he hoisted Freddy up and over so that he was standing in the snow on the edge of a parking lot. Vaulting the ledge, David reached down again and, with one mug in each hand, motioned with his chin towards his car.

Together they hobbled, skated, slid to David's car and got into the front seat. Freddy sat where a driver would, while David sat beside him, opening the glove compartment. He pulled out a white tin box with blue and red markings on it, and opened it. Their chocolate sat solidly on the dashboard.

"O.K.," said David, "put your chin up and grit your teeth."

Freddy did as he was told. David cleansed the wound, dabbing it with some liquid that stung, but only for a moment. Then he put three Band-Aids on Freddy's chin—two across the cut, almost ear to ear, and one up and down to keep the first two secure.

"There," said David. "That should do it."

"Thank you," said Freddy.

"I wouldn't say you've lost a pint of blood, but maybe it would be a good idea to sit here a minute, Moose, resting." He handed Freddy's mug to him. Together they sipped the chocolate. "Good stuff, eh, Moose?" David said.

"You know a lot about fucking?" Freddy asked quickly and quietly.

26

David blinked. "Well," he said, "I *think* so. Why?"

"Well," said Freddy, "my dad just told me about it. But I think he forgot something."

"What?"

"How a man's penis does it."

"Does what?"

"Gets in."

"Oh," David said. He looked out across the pond, holding his cup of chocolate just below his mouth, not drinking from it. "Did your dad tell you about the sperm and the egg?" David asked after a moment.

Freddy nodded. "He said it's called, sometimes, sleeping with people."

David smiled. Then he looked puzzled. He put his cup on the dashboard and looked as though he were concentrating on some distant, hard-to-grasp thought. Suddenly he laughed. "You know what,

Moose? I was just remembering how my dad told me about sex. I think he forgot the same thing yours did."

Freddy smiled for the first time since he'd fallen. His chin felt oddly tight so he stopped smiling right away, afraid of tearing the bandage off or maybe starting the bleeding again.

"Now that I think of it," David said, edging around to face Freddy more directly, "I'm almost certain of it. He didn't tell you about . . . about being aroused?"

"What does that mean?" asked Freddy.

"Well," began his friend, "that's what happens before anyone begins having sex."

"But what is it?" Freddy asked again. Then, before David had a chance to answer that question, Freddy fired another. "Have you ever done it?"

David grinned. It seemed to Freddy that he was remembering something. "Yes, Fred," he said, "I have."

Freddy nodded his head. It was O.K., then, he decided. At least he would be getting information again from someone who knew what he was talking about.

27

There was a pause. Freddy wanted to tell David to go ahead, to get started. But David seemed to be thinking about what he had to say. His mouth was open as though to speak, but his lips weren't moving. Freddy heard the shouts and laughter from the ice in back of him and wanted, sort of, to turn around and see what was happening.

"First, Fred," David said finally, "there are a lot of things you *feel* before you actually get to bed with a girl."

"Like what?"

"Lots of little things that really don't have names. I mean, there are some girls you don't want to sleep with. And there are some you do. It could be because the girl is pretty. Maybe it's because she laughs a way you like. It could be how her ankles are shaped, or the size of her breasts."

Freddy waited, holding his cup of chocolate

tightly both for warmth and because he felt a little nervous in the face of the final word.

"Anyway, sometimes you meet girls you sort of .. . well, you *feel* something for."

"How?"

"You get funny inside," David said. "Your stomach maybe jumps around. Or your mind starts picturing certain things. Anyway, there is a kind of pull between you and her, something that seems to tie you both together. Maybe your eyes meet accidentally and without any words you both know you like each other a lot."

Freddy frowned. This seemed to be taking an awfully long time.

"Sometimes," David went on, "you spend a lot of time with the girl, getting to know her. Other times you don't have to. You feel you already know her and that everything will make sense when it happens."

Freddy concentrated on watching David, since what he heard didn't seem to be getting any nearer to what he wanted to know. David was smiling as he spoke. He seemed to be remembering all sorts of things he didn't mention out loud. He looked out through the window behind Freddy, and Freddy, without turning around to see where David's look was directed, knew he was watching Tina at the edge of the ice. David's eyes seemed to brighten and he began pushing his long blond hair back from his forehead.

David wasn't nervous exactly, Freddy decided. But he did seem to think that fucking was something more special than Freddy's father did. Freddy remembered his father's saying it was something everyone did. David seemed to think it was something wonderful that only happened every so often.

"Anyway," David continued, "suddenly your mind lets go and your emotions—your heart, I guess —take over. You begin to like the girl more and more. And fucking is one way of showing how you feel."

Freddy could tell David was working up to something at last.

"So, Fred," said David, holding up his hand, "what happens is this. Your penis gets stiff."

David's hand had become a fist and then just as suddenly a finger uncurled and straightened out, pointing into the air. Freddy was nodding. He had been right after all! "It sort of tells you what you already knew—that you would like to get inside the girl so you can be really, truly together."

Freddy's eyes opened a bit wider. Being together was an idea he hadn't considered.

"And Fred." David rushed on, "that's about
the most wonderful thing in the whole world, being
together. You feel as though you and she can solve
any problem, make a real difference in the world.
You're sharing something so exciting, so new that
even after it's over, you can think about it and talk
about it and it takes on all kinds of meanings and
messages. For that's really what making love is,
sending dif—"

"I never heard it called that," interrupted
Freddy.

"Well," said David, "that's about the nicest
way of putting it. And if you're lucky all your life,
Fred, that's what fucking will be: making love with
someone you really do love."

Freddy thought this over. "Where was I?"
David asked.

"Stiff," said Freddy.

"Oh. Right. Well, when your penis gets stiff,
you can see how easy it would be to put it into a girl,
can't you? You just push a little and you're in."

David opened his car door. A gust of cool air

circulated around the pair, seeming to push the warmer, closer air out and away again from the car. David put his right leg out of the car. "Is that all you wanted to know, Moose?"

"I guess," said Freddy, his hand on his door handle, too. "Except how you get out."

David smiled. "You could answer that if you thought a minute, Fred. Your penis gets soft again, and you simply pull back out."

David unfolded himself and stood outside the car. "Wait!" shouted Freddy across the front seat. David leaned back into the car. "Is it fun?" asked Freddy. "My dad says it is, but he wasn't very clear about why."

David grinned at Freddy and half sat, half knelt at the corner of the front seat. "Part of the fun, Fred, is sharing the experience. How did your dad say it was?"

"Like a tingle," reported Freddy.

"That's fair enough. Because when you're making love, being inside is O.K., but it's the movement you make before sending out your sperm that gives you, and gives your girl, real pleasure. Or fun, if you want to call it that. The sensation of fucking, Fred, is fun."

"What kind of movement?" Freddy wanted to know, slamming the car door behind him. David crossed in front of the car and, step by careful step, the two crossed the parking lot towards the ice.

"Don't you worry about that, Fred. You'll know how to do it when the time comes." David chuckled a little and waved at Tina. Freddy smiled, too, and then, again, remembered his wound. He stopped smiling.

"When will it be?" he asked David. "When will the time come?"

"You can't rush it, Fred," David told him. "You'll get there. Everyone does, sooner or later."

"Next year?"

"No, I wouldn't think so. Listen, Fred, it could be, but I doubt it. More likely a few years from now." David dropped down over the stone ledge to the ice. He turned around and lifted Freddy down, too, steadying him on his skates as he did so. "But don't worry," he said to Freddy. "You'll know."

David looked around the rink, lifting first one leg and then the other from the ice, flexing, to get ready for a headlong dash into the crowd. His hand was on Freddy's shoulder, but his eyes were running out and past and through the skaters. "In the meantime, Fred," David said, "there are all kinds of things you can be doing, things you already know how to do better than almost anyone else." .

David turned and looked directly down at Freddy. He was smiling. He reached out and messed up Freddy's hair. Freddy swung back at David playfully. "Come on, Moose!" David called as he skated towards the center of the pond. "You can have plenty of fun while you're waiting!"

Freddy watched David's tall figure bend forward for speed as he raced across the ice, tagging one boy and then another as he passed. His path along the surface could have been traced by the happy shouts that followed him. Freddy just stood sturdily on the ice, watching.

What David had told him, besides answering his question, sounded pretty good. He wasn't clear exactly about the excitement both David and his father felt belonged to making love. But they did both think it was super. Freddy decided he would, too, when his own time came. But now that he knew what he knew, he wished he didn't have to wait so long.

Freddy spied Johnny making his shaky way across the ice on the other side of the pond.

He pushed off easily into the crowds, remembering to be a little more careful than usual because of his chin.

Freddy decided he wouldn't tell Johnny what he knew now about making love. He sounded the phrase over in his mind. *Making love.* He decided he liked it much better than the word he had first seen on the wall in the boys' washroom. Let Johnny Norman figure out the difference. Let him find out for himself, since he was so smart.

Freddy's speed increased. Johnny precariously made his way through other skaters, sometimes reaching out to grab one for balance, and then letting go again when he felt secure. He didn't even look towards where Freddy was.

The wind flew by Freddy's ears. He opened his mouth in a grin. He felt the pull of the bandages. *Nuts!* he decided. That was nothing to worry about.

He sailed by two little boys, hanging on to each other for support. Freddy cut around them and stood up a little, feeling tall.

In spite of Pru, even though he was short for his age *now,* Freddy just knew, he suddenly *believed,* he was absolutely certain that one day he would grow.

In the meantime, what could be more fun than knowing something Johnny Norman didn't? Maybe, just every once in a while, Freddy would hint a little. Just a little. It would drive Johnny crazy!

He was a young cat, but strong, and in his left ear he wore a tiny golden earring . . .

RAMA THE GYPSY CAT

by Betsy Byars

illustrated by Peggy Bacon

Rama loved the gypsy woman, and the gypsy woman loved him. But when the caravan went on, Rama was somehow left behind. So Rama set off on his own to face danger and adventures which led him to fight with a vicious wharf cat, a terrifying ride down a raging, flooded river, and a long weary, hungry journey on foot in search of his home.

An Avon Camelot Book
41608 $1.25

Also by Betsy Byars
AFTER THE GOAT MAN   41590 $1.25
THE MIDNIGHT FOX   46987 $1.50
THE SUMMER OF THE SWANS   50526 $1.75
TROUBLE RIVER   47001 $1.50
THE WINGED COLT OF CASA MIA   46995 $1.50

When the white whale called to her, Marian had to answer . . .

THE SELCHIE'S SEED

by Shulamith Oppenheim

illustrated by Diane Goode

She heard the call from the sea and she knew that she must answer it. It came from a strange power, greater than any on earth. It cast a spell that neither her mother, her father, nor her brother could help her break.

Marian knew the wondrous magic of the Selchie that summoned her was an ancient heritage from the past. She would accept it as one had to accept the power of an enchantment.

An Avon Camelot Book
34165 $1.25

A suspenseful mystery with a surprise ending!

THE CHRISTMAS TREE MYSTERY

by Wylly Folk St. John

Beth Carlton was in trouble. She accused Pete Abel of steal-
ing the Christmas ornaments from her family tree, something
she knew he hadn't done. And what was worse—the police
believed her! Beth had two days to prove to the police that
Pete wasn't a thief, and all she had to go on was her step-
brother's word that Pete was innocent.

An Avon Camelot Book
46300 $1.50

THE REAL ME
by Betty Miles

"My book is not the kind that tells 'How Tomboy Mindy discovered that growing up gracefully can be as fun as playing baseball.'

"I have often thought how relaxing it would be to be invisible. But when I took over Richard's paper route they said 'girls can't deliver papers.' And when I wanted to take tennis instead of slimnastics, they said 'girls like to do graceful feminine things.' So I had to speak out. I only wanted things to be fair.

"My book is for anyone who might want to read about the life and thoughts of a person like me. If some boy wants to read this, go ahead. Maybe you will learn something."

An Avon Camelot Book
48199 $1.50

"Harold waited to see if he could catch sight of that glint of steel he was always hearing about. The gun barrel. He thought of how he must look standing there, fat and pale and scared. The perfect target . . ."

AFTER THE GOAT MAN

by Betsy Byars

illustrated by Ronald Himler

When Harold played Monopoly with Ada and Figgy, he always won. He could make his voice sound deep and important on the phone. And he had a WCLG Golden Oldie T-shirt. But nothing could make up for the fact that he was fat. Harold thought he was the most miserable person in the world, until the night that Figgy's eccentric grandfather picked up a shotgun and disappeared.

Then, when Figgy was badly injured in an accident, it was suddenly up to Harold to find the Goat Man. And on the way, he discovered that his problems were very small compared with the problems of other people.

An Avon Camelot Book
41590 $1.25

Also by Betsy Byars
THE SUMMER OF THE SWANS   50526 $1.75
THE MIDNIGHT FOX   46987 $1.50
RAMA THE GYPSY CAT   41608 $1.25
TROUBLE RIVER   47001 $1.50
THE WINGED COLT OF CASA MIA   46995 $1.50

Gilly Ground was an orphan and all he wanted was a little peace and quiet . . .

DORP DEAD

by Julia Cunningham

illustrated by James Spanfeller

Life in the orphanage was difficult in many ways. Gilly spent as much time as he could in the abandoned tower in the woods. It was peaceful there—and it was there that Gilly met the Hunter. Then, one day, he was placed in a foster home. And Gilly felt as though he were trapped in a nightmare come true.

An Avon Camelot Book
51458 $1.95

Also by Julia Cunningham
DEAR RAT   46615 $1.50

An old mansion, a graveyard, and a mysterious skull!

UNCLE ROBERT'S SECRET

by Wylly Folk St. John

"You don't know what scared is till you've fallen out of a tree late at night into a bunch of broken-down gravestones, practically on top of somebody you think might be a mean guy . . . and there's an awful scream still ringing in your ears."

Bob should have known how hard it would be to keep a secret, especially when that secret happened to be a bedraggled little boy named Tim. And when Bob finally shared it with his brother and sister, they suddenly found themselves involved in a very spooky mystery.

An Avon Camelot Book
46326 $1.50